$\mathcal{S}$omeone has sent me another copy of my picture, and I can't help but stare at it. On my big computer screen, it's incredibly clear. I'm amazed that it's me. I touch my mouth, the way you touch your mouth after you've been kissed, the way I did when Luke first kissed me at Ash's party at the end of the summer. I can still taste the salt on my tongue, but I can't connect the picture to me.

Also by
Laura Ruby

LILY'S GHOSTS
THE WALL AND THE WING
THE CHAOS KING

Good Girls

Laura Ruby

HARPER TEEN

An Imprint of HarperCollins*Publishers*

HarperTeen is an imprint of HarperCollins Publishers.

Good Girls
Copyright © 2006 by Laura Ruby
All rights reserved. Printed in the United States of America.
www.harperteen.com

Ruby, Laura.
    Good girls / Laura Ruby.—1st ed.
        p.   cm.
    Summary: Sixteen-year-old high school senior Audrey is humiliated
when a compromising photograph of her is sent around her school,
but she discovers a toughness within her that she never knew she had.
    ISBN 978-0-06-088225-9
    [1. Interpersonal relations—Fiction.   2. Sex—Fiction.
3. Conduct of life—Fiction.   4. High schools—Fiction.
5. Schools—Fiction.]   I. Title.
PZ7.R83138Go 2006   2006000340
[Fic]—dc22   CIP
                                                                  AC

Typography by Amy Ryan
❖
First HarperTeen paperback edition, 2008

*For all my girls . . .
and for everyone else's*

". . . it took me too long to realize
that i don't take good pictures
cuz i have the kind of beauty
that moves"
—Ani DiFranco, "Evolve"

Good Girls

Good Girls

Beg Me

*A*sh says she's the Dark Queen of the Damned. I say I'm the Empress of the Undead.

My dad, passing by the bathroom where we're getting ready, takes one look and declares us Two Weird Girls from Jersey.

"That'll work," Ash says.

Tonight, we're Goth. We've got the layers of black

mesh shirts, the cargo pants rolled up to the knees, the ripped fishnets, the combat boots, the white face makeup and the smudgy rings of eyeliner. Ash brought a can of black hair spray, but she's already used most of it on her curly brown hair. "Not sure if there's enough left for you, Rapunzel."

"Shut up and start spraying," I say. My hair is blond, and long enough to tuck into the back of my cargoes. Ash blackens the strands around my face and puts skunky streaks all around the back. The noise scares Cat Stevens—aka Stevie, The Furminator, and Mr. Honey Head—who is watching us from his perch on the toilet tank. He jumps down and dashes out of the bathroom.

"What did you do to Stevie?" my mom calls. I hear her murmuring, "Poor baby kitty. Little marmalade man."

After Ash finishes, we crowd the mirror. "We are so hot," she says. And we are. Dark and freaky and brooding, the way vampires might look. I should like it more than I do. My black bra doesn't fit right, and the straps dig into my shoulders. The fishnets itch. It's a stupidly warm night, and I'm already sweating. Plus, I've got on so much mascara that when I blink, my lashes spike my skin.

It's different for Ash. She's sort of Goth-y anyway, with her pierced eyebrow and sharp cheekbones and the German swearwords courtesy of her *Deutsch* grandma.

I lean closer to the mirror. "I should have bought contacts. In the store, I saw these green lenses with slanted pupils, kind of like a lizard."

Ash frowns. "You have the coolest eyes on the planet. Amber."

"Right," I say. "Like that stuff insects get caught in."

"Plus," she says, ignoring me, "you don't get contacts for one Halloween party." Ash blinks her own dark eyes, lush as melted chocolate. "And you can stop being so cranky, please."

"Sorry." I bite my lip. "Can you believe this is our last Halloween together?"

Ash's hands fly up. "Enough with the 'Can you believe this is our last whatever?' stuff. It's *October*. We've got like eight whole months of school left."

"More like seven."

"Seven, then."

"Six if you count vacations," I say.

"Audrey, the key word is 'months.' Besides," she says, digging her elbow into my side, "there are more important things to worry about right now."

"Like what?"

"Like a certain person by the name of Luke DeSalvio, who I'm sure will be at Joelle's tonight. You remember him."

"Oh," I say. "Right."

"Listen to her!" says Ash. "*Oh, right*. Like you aren't

about to explode all over this bathroom."

"Yeah, well. Like you're always reminding me, it's not serious. We're just friends," I say.

"With benefits," says Ash, her voice low so my parents can't hear it. "Anyone for tongue sushi?"

I smile but don't answer. This is Ash, the girl whose name is always mentioned in the same breath as mine: AshandAudrey, AudreyandAsh. But there's so much I haven't told her, and now I don't even know where to start. What I do know: me and Luke aren't friends, me and Luke aren't anything. I had decided I would tell him this tonight, if the subject ever came up. But we never did do much talking.

"There will be lots of guys at the party," I say. "Who knows? Maybe I'll branch out a little."

"Really?" Ash says. "Well, well. I guess someone's got a brain in her head after all."

Her phone bleats like a sheep and she grabs for it, looks at the screen. "Picture mail," she says. She presses a few buttons and the image pops up. "My baby brother in his Spider-Man costume."

I look over her shoulder. "Cute."

"Please. The boy's a demon from hell. Last week, he actually peed in one of the houseplants." Ash tosses the phone back on the sink and shakes her head in the mirror. "The spray looks great on you, but it makes my hair look like ramen noodles."

That makes me laugh a little. "Squid-ink ramen noodles," I say.

"You have to get your parents to take you to normal restaurants once in a while. Pizza, anyone?"

"We go out for pizza. Of course, it's the kind with a cornmeal crust and gobs of goat cheese."

"Goats!" says Ash.

My not-quite-normal parents are waiting for us in the living room with two glasses of wine and a digital camera—the wine for them, the camera for us. Usually, I hate all the pictures. I don't need anyone documenting my awkward teenage years. Tonight my dad insists and for once I'm okay with it, maybe because I don't look much like me anymore. My dad has us pose on the antique church pew against the yellow wall. He backs up and almost falls over the coffee table. My mom laughs and takes a sip of wine, shining and velvet in the light. They love this part, the part when I'm getting ready to go out but I haven't left yet. I wonder if it will be hard for them when I'm off at college. Besides Cat Stevens, I'm all they've got.

"Okay, girls," my dad says. "Look Gothic!"

"Goth, Dad," I say. "Not Goth*ic*."

"Sorry," he says. "Ready? Say 'Goat cheese!'"

Because it's my dad, we both yell "Goat cheese!" In the picture, we've got the black hair, the white skin, and the bruise-colored lips, but we're both grinning like five-year-olds. Ash takes one look at the picture and says, "We've got to work on our attitudes, girl. We've got to think dark thoughts."

"Oh?" says my mom, intrigued. "What kind of dark thoughts?" She writes mystery novels, but the cozy kind with sweet old ladies, little baby kitties, and lots of homemade cookies. Oh, and a murder or two. Death by knitting needles. Dark thoughts in sunshiny places.

Ash is doing her best to look creepy. "Madness," she says. "Mayhem. Malice."

I try to think of a dark thought, but the best I can come up with is mixed-up, sad stuff—Luke stuff, our-last-Halloween-ever stuff. I don't mention it, though. I'm already an Empress of the Undead. I don't need to kill everything else off, too.

After the pictures, my mom makes me promise to take my cell, which she seems to think will protect me from car accidents and evil, drunken boys bent on stealing my virtue. *Yes, I'll take the cell. Yes, I'll call if I need anything.* We say good-bye and we're out the door. Ash has to drive because I'm still too young. I skipped a grade in grammar school, and now I'm the only senior without a license. Doesn't help that the driving age in New Jersey is seventeen, probably the oldest in the country. At least my parents let me stay out as late as everyone else. I might be sixteen and three quarters, but my mom says I'm an old soul. Lately, I've been feeling like one. As we get closer to Joelle's, I start to get this nervous flutter in my stomach that gets more fluttery with each block. I cross my fingers and whisper a teeny little prayer in my head: *Please, God, do not let me make an idiot of myself tonight. Let me have a little fun.*

It takes a while to find a parking spot, because everyone goes to Joelle's Halloween parties. She's had them every year since the seventh grade. Only strangers or losers show up without costumes, because they'll be forced to wear one of Joelle's tutus from her dancing days. When Ash and I walk in the door, I see only one guy with a tutu, a big fluffy pink one. He looks totally stupid, but that's the point.

Joelle runs up to us, almost tripping over her long white dress. "Look at you guys!" Joelle shrieks. "You're *so* scary!" Joelle is dressed up as a goddess or whatever, with the gauzy dress and the gold armbands, shimmer powder on her face and these long curls in front of her ears. Ash says that Joelle always wears something that will make her look pretty rather than freaky. Joelle would never dress up as a mummy or a monster, or even a Goth chick. Joelle likes to look like Joelle, only more sparkly.

"So who are you?" Ash says.

"What do you mean, who am I?" Joelle shrieks. She's

a shrieker, especially when there's a crowd. "I'm that tragic Greek heroine, Antigone!"

"Anti what?" says Ash.

Joelle puts her hands on her hips and stamps her foot. "Antigone!"

"Antifreeze?" says Ash.

"Antacid," I say. "Ant Spray."

"Get thee to a theater," Joelle says. Joelle wants to be an actress. Joelle *is* an actress. Her mother has already pulled her out of school a bunch of times to do commercials, an off-off-off Broadway play, and a spot on *Law & Order*.

Ash raises eyebrows that we'd darkened with pencil. "You guys spend enough time at the theater, okay? Besides, you don't look like a tragic Greek heroine as much as you look like an extra from *Lord of the Rings*."

"You suck," says Joelle, punching her in the arm.

"Who sucks?" Luke says. He walks over to where we're standing in the hallway. He's wearing black pants and a black shirt with a white paper collar. I suddenly feel like there's not enough oxygen to go around.

"What's up, Father?" I say.

He puts a hand on the top of my head. "My child, you are a sinner."

Ash snorts. "You should know."

"Hey," says Luke. "I'm not a priest, I'm a pastor. Pastors are allowed."

"Allowed what?" I say. Luke grins and my face goes hot. I'm glad that it's dark and that I'm wearing the white makeup. But Luke can tell anyway. He grins even wider before he drifts off into the crowd again. My head feels warm where his hand was, like he's excited my hair follicles. This is how I am around him. My brains dribble right out of my ear and I'm left with nothing but a body I can barely control. I'm actually a little surprised when my legs don't scuttle after him and fling me at his feet. It's happened before.

"He's so cute," says Joelle. "You guys are still, like, hanging out, right?"

"Depends," I say. I watch as Luke starts talking to Pam Markovitz, who is dressed up like some kind of junkyard cat, chewed-looking ears and whiskers and everything. Luke reaches out and yanks her bedraggled tail. Again my dumb, brainless body reacts: hands contract to fists, stomach clenches as if around bad chicken.

Joelle sees where I'm looking. "Slut."

"I heard that Pam gave Jay Epstein head at the movies the other night," Ash says.

"Really?" I say. "Who said that?"

"Jay Epstein."

"There's a reputable source," I say.

"Still," says Joelle. "Everyone knows she's been with, like, the entire planet."

"What an unpleasant visual," says Ash. "Gotta love

how the leotard rides up her butt."

"Luke doesn't seem to mind," says Joelle. She catches my face. "I mean, he's really really hot, but it's a good thing you guys aren't boyfriend/girlfriend and all that."

"Oh, please. Who needs a boyfriend?" says Ash. "It's not like we're gonna get married anytime soon. Anyway, like Audrey keeps saying, college is right around the corner."

It's not supposed to bug me that Luke's such a player, everything's supposed to be casual. But in our friends-with-benefits arrangement, it seems like he's the one who gets all the benefits. "Any other hot guys here?" I ask.

"I hope so," Ash says. "I haven't hooked up in weeks."

Joelle runs off to get us some "soda," which means that there's beer that we'll have to hide from Joelle's dad, who probably won't come out of his office over the garage long enough to see anything anyway. Me and Ash follow Joelle into the den. All the usuals are there: hoboes, witches, devils, football players dressed like cheerleaders, cheerleaders dressed like football players. "So original," says Ash. There *is* a guy wearing a plaid jacket with a fish tank on his head. When we ask, he says, "I'm swimming with the fishies." Red plastic fish are glued to the walls of the tank. His teeth make a white piano in his blue-painted face.

Almost immediately, Ash starts dragging me over to every reasonably cute guy who doesn't already know us from school. Joelle runs around taking bad pictures with her digital camera. Luke goes from girl to girl, stealing witch hats and pretending to poke people with a pitchfork he's stolen from one of the devils. As if it's my fault that everyone thinks she's a slut, Pam Markovitz huddles with Cindy Terlizzi on the couch, Cindy shooting dirty looks and Pam smirking at me. I ignore them, talking to this person and that person, trying to relax and have a good time, but I feel like I'm far away and watching everything on a TV screen. Ash is getting sick of me being so gloomy, so she flirts big-time with Fish Tank, looking to hook up. At random intervals, cell phones ring and jingle and sing, and people go all yellular, shouting over the music, *"What? WHAT?"*

I down the rest of my beer and go over to the cooler for another one. I don't even like beer.

"Awwww. Why so sad? Where's Mr. Popularity?"

I turn and see Chilly. He's wearing baggy jeans, high-tops, and a T-shirt that says "Insert Lame Costume Here." Apparently it was good enough for Joelle, because he's not wearing a tutu.

"Who?" I say.

"You know who," he says.

"I don't," I say. Chilly gives me the creeps. He has eyes like radioactive algae and a wormy mouth. We learned a word for wormy in biology. *Anneloid.*

"I'm surprised to see you here," he says. "Don't you have a few thousand tests to study for? Another foreign language to learn?"

"Croatian," I say. "But I can do that tomorrow."

"You are such a good, good girl. Doesn't it kill you that you aren't graduating number one?"

As of the end of last year, I was number four in our class and had to work my butt off to get that much. A lot of people think that I'm some kind of genius because I skipped a grade, but I don't think I'm much smarter than anyone else. I'm just weirder.

"There's eight months to graduation," I say. "Anything can happen."

"Nah," he says. He takes a sip of his drink, not beer but ginger ale. "You'll never catch up with Ron. He's got everyone beat. And Kimberly would rather commit ritual suicide than let anyone take her number two. I forget who's number three, but whoever it is, you won't budge them."

"You sleep through all your classes. What do you care?"

"I don't care at all. My test scores will get me where I want to go."

"Oh, I'm sure they will," I say. I resist the urge to puke on his shoes. I cannot *believe* that I ever went out with him. I want to jam my finger into my ear and scratch the memory out of my brain.

He takes a step closer to me, his algae eyes scraping across my chest. "Wanna hook up?"

"No," I say.

"Come on," he says. "You're free, I'm free."

I think, *You're always free.* I look around the room for Luke. A mistake, because Chilly snorts.

"Don't worry about him. He's already occupied." Chilly touches my cheek with a sandpapery fingertip. "He won't mind sharing."

I slap his hand and walk away. I can hear Chilly laughing behind me, and I wish I'd thrown my beer in his face or something dramatic like that. But the drama queen stuff is Joelle's job, not mine, and Chilly knows it. It's why he likes to bother me.

When I'm upstairs in the bathroom, I swig the beer and check my makeup in the harsh light. I look like the Empress of the Undead, if Empresses of the Undead are pouty and pathetic. What's the use of planning a big breakup if the person you're breaking up with is too busy yanking on tails and poking people with pitchforks? I suddenly do not want to be at this party at all. I wonder if I should call my mom and ask for a ride home.

I'm still trying to decide when I bump into Luke in the hallway. Before I know what's up, he's pulled me into one of the bedrooms and shut the door with his foot.

"Hey," I say.

"Hey yourself," he says. He—or someone else—has taken off the white collar, so he's all in black. He looks more devilish than the devils do. I think that if there is a real devil, he has golden hair and round blue angel eyes, just like Luke.

"What?" he says, because I'm staring.

"Nothing," I say. "Look. I've got to go."

"Come on! We haven't even had a chance to hang out yet."

"That's because there are too many other kitties around here," I say.

"You're not jealous," he says.

I roll my eyes, hard. He has one hand around my upper arm and he squeezes. He's smiling, and I hate him for just a second. As usual, it passes.

"Let go," I tell him.

"Is something wrong?"

I sigh. Everything is wrong. Maybe it's the beer. Note to self: ~~beer.~~

"Have I told you how amazing you look tonight?" he says.

I know when I'm being played, but the compliment cheers me anyway—that's what kind of dork I am. "Thanks," I tell him. He leans down to kiss me and I pull away. "I don't think that's a good idea."

Surprise. "Why not?"

"Just 'cause, okay?"

He doesn't believe me. *I* don't believe me. My body is practically squealing with happiness. I'm sure he can hear it.

He tries to kiss me again and I turn my face. "What's the matter?" he says, concerned for real now. His hand falls away from my arm.

"I've been meaning to tell you." I take a deep breath. "I don't want to do this anymore."

"Do what?"

"What we're doing."

He doesn't answer. He tips his head and seems genuinely perplexed. It pisses me off.

"I don't want to do *what we do*. I don't want to . . ." I look for the right words. "I don't want to be involved with anyone right now."

He frowns—blinking, quiet. "But I thought we were cool," he says, finally. "I thought we were just hanging out."

"Hanging out. Yeah, I love that," I say. What I don't say: *I love that we've hooked up at every party every weekend for the last two and a half months but somehow we're not involved. I love that we go to the same school but I don't get much more than a "hey" in the hallways, no matter how many times your tongue has been down my throat.*

Of course, since I don't actually finish the thought, since I haven't said anything like it before, he has no clue what I'm talking about. I stand there, watching the expressions march across his face. I can imagine what he's thinking: *Did she just say something about LOVE? Does this mean we can't hook up? Should I hook up with Pam Markovitz instead? What's going on???*

I almost feel bad for him. That's what devils do, they make you feel bad.

I must be staring again, because Luke's frown smoothes out. He's got these perfect lips, full and pink. Pretty girl lips on a boy's rough, stubbled face. I can't help it, I think it's hot. And he's so close I can smell him. Warm and clean and sort of soapy-spicy. It's a great smell. It's a smell that can make you drunk. I wonder if I am. Can almost two beers make you drunk?

His frown is totally gone now, and mine must be gone, too, because he ignores what I said, reels me in, and kisses me. I feel the press of his chest and the weight of his arm around my waist, all those heavy bones, and I think: *Okay, fine. But this is it. After this, no more dumb high school hookups with dumb high school boys, no matter how hot or soapy-smelling they are. I'm done with this. Done.*

Maybe because he can sense it, or because he's afraid I'll change my mind, Luke takes his time, lips barely touching, barely brushing mine. The music thumping downstairs plays a heartbeat under my feet as the kiss goes from sweet to serious—slidey and sideways and deep. Like always, a thousand flowers bloom in my gut, my skin tingles everywhere, and my brains sidle toward the door.

I don't know how much time goes by before his fingers are crawling under my various shirts and he's pushing me backwards toward the bed. Another not-so-good idea. On the bed, he could work me up, peel off all the layers till there's nothing left to cover me and it's too hard to say no.

I say, "No."

He mumbles something against my collarbone, something beginning with "I—I want, I need, I-I-I." It makes me so mad. Isn't it enough that I turn into some sort of panting, slobbering wolf-girl when he's around? I should let him see all of me? Have all of me? Just because he wants it?

I plant my feet and steer him around. I put my hands on his shoulders and sit him down on the edge of the mattress.

"What?" he says.

"Shut up."

I drop down in front of him. I can't make him listen or understand or care, and I don't even want to. But I want to do something. Make him feel me. Make him beg me. Make him be the naked one.

And so, I do.

With Luke's low groan in my ears and my eyes shutting out the world, I don't hear the door open behind us, I don't see the flash of light.

The Photograph

*A*sh is not a morning person. She is also

not a neat person.

When I get in her car on Monday morning, there

are old Styrofoam coffee cups strewn on the floor

and one attached to her lips. Sheets of paper,

crumpled napkins, and random changes

of clothes—fresh and foul—litter the backseat.

Sticking to the dashboard is a quarter of a glazed donut, age indeterminate. Me and Ash have been friends since the sixth grade and she's been driving me to school since the day she got her license, so I'm used to her morning-fog face, her bloodshot eyes, her endless coffee, and the disgusting mess that is her personal universe. It's not even so disgusting anymore. I grab a handful of napkins and bravely peel the donut off the dashboard and dump it in the ashtray, which is filled with butts from Ash's on-again, off-again smoking habit.

I don't say anything for a few minutes, waiting until Ash has more caffeine in her system. After a while, she grumbles, "What are you so happy about?" She pumps the gas pedal of her old Dodge to keep it from dying out at the stoplight.

"Who says I'm happy?" I ask her.

"Because you're not complaining about the dumb party or the itchy costume or how long it took you to get the makeup off or the fourteen thousand college essays you had to write yesterday," she says. "That means you're happy about something."

Ash is not happy. Fish Tank, she'd told me on the way home from the party, had some girlfriend who went to the Catholic high school, so didn't want to hook up with Ash or anyone else. I didn't tell her about ending it with Luke. For some reason, it had felt like a secret, something that was more special because I was the only one in the world who knew it, or at least the only one in the world who knew I was serious about it. Sunday morning, I sat in church while the pastor—the *really* boring one—babbled on about some dumb movie he saw and what Jesus might think of it, going on so much and so long that he seemed to be putting himself and the rest of us to sleep. So instead of listening to Pastor Narcolepsy, I told God what happened (yeah, yeah, as if she didn't know already). Anyway, I said that it was over and that I was okay. I said I felt strong, like I'd broken a spell. I swore that I would concentrate on my work again, that I would be back to myself. I would no longer be operating in a Luke-induced lust haze. I would be myself again.

But with the harsh Monday-morning light piercing my eyes, with Ash mumbling like an old drunk into her coffee, I decide to go public.

"I'm not exactly happy," I say. "But I feel really good. I broke up with Luke on Saturday night."

"You did what?"

"I broke up with Luke."

Her mouth hangs open. Then she says, "How can you break up with a guy if you're not even going out with him?"

This annoys me. "We've been hooking up for the last two and a half months, Ash. We were doing *something*. And now we're not."

"Right," says Ash. She jams her coffee cup into the cup holder. "Ten bucks says you'll change your mind."

"I'm not going to change my mind." I check myself as I say this, wondering if I'm telling the truth. But I am. I feel it. At the party, as Luke was buttoning up his shirt over that body, a body so perfect that it was like a punch to the throat, I'd said, "Well, it's been fun. 'Bye. Have a nice life," and walked out of the bedroom without looking back. "I just don't want it anymore, that's all," I say.

"Can you hear yourself?" she says. "You don't want *Luke DeSalvio*. Everybody wants Luke DeSalvio. Hell, if you guys kept hooking up, maybe he'd ask you to the prom."

"I'm not going to keep hooking up with some random guy in case the cheerleading squad isn't available to escort him to the prom."

"Bite my head off, why don't you?" She drums her fingers on the steering wheel. "He's not exactly random. I thought you liked him. I thought you more than liked him."

I sigh. "I do. I did. I can't figure out if I wanted him or I just wanted, well. . . ,"

"You dog!"

"That's the point. I'm not. I'd like to be able to talk to the person I'm hooking up with."

"*Talk?* To a guy? What for?" She sees my face and

laughs. "Kidding, kidding." She digs around underneath the donut for a still-smokable butt, giving up when she doesn't find one. "I guess I'm just surprised. I mean, I think it's totally the right decision. It's great. It does say something that he went for you, though, as much as I hate to say it."

"Thanks a lot," I say.

"You know what I mean," she says. "You, Miss Skip-a-Grade, 9.45 GPA, off-to-the-Ivy-League prodigy—"

"I wish you would stop saying that."

"And him with the bazillion varsity letters, the golden tan, and the . . ."

"Amazing ass?"

Ash pulls an I'm-so-shocked face and adopts her British accent. "Such a *cheeky* girl!"

"Such a dorky girl," I say. "Who knows why he was hanging out with me. Maybe I was next on the list." I reach back and rebundle the hair at the back of my head, thankfully blond again. "I tried the casual hookup thing. It's not for me. It's like I was trying to be someone else. Trying to be him."

Ash considers this. "I'm not sure that's such a bad idea. To try to be like guys. Look at them. They just do whatever they want and nobody cares. Why shouldn't we be like them?"

I sigh. This is not the Ash I've known forever. The Ash I knew used to be totally and completely in love with Jimmy—poet, guitar guy, future rock star. They went out for a year and a half, until he had some sort of schizoid butthead attack and cheated on her with a freshman girl with shiny Barbie hair and enormous Barbie breasts. Since then, it's all she thinks about. How free guys are. How they go after what they want, how they get it, how happy they are doing it. How hooking up is so much better than having a boyfriend, how it can keep you from getting hurt.

But I know that's not true, and I know better than to bring up Jimmy. After Jimmy, Ashley became Ash and Jimmy became a ghost. He might as well be dead, even though his locker is right down the hall from ours. "This particular prodigy doesn't have time for Luke DeSalvio or any other guy," I say. "This prodigy has to keep her grades up so that the colleges come knocking with the big bucks."

Ash smiles. "My list is up to six now. I've got Rutgers, Oberlin, NYU, SUNY, Sarah Lawrence. I'm hoping that they'll ignore my math grades. And my chemistry grades. And that D I got in cooking freshman year."

"I still don't know how you managed a D in cooking."

"Mrs. Hooper had us make mayonnaise. How is that cooking?"

"You said six colleges."

"I'm also applying to Cornell." She gives me a knowing look. "Bet that's your safe school."

I pull Ash's cup out of the holder and take a swig of cold, gritty coffee. "Nothing's safe."

First-period study, and Chilly's on an Audrey hunt. He lopes into the library and gives me a wicked grin. He sits in the seat across from me, his brows waggling, suggestive of God knows what. I ignore him, grab one of my books, and flip it open without really seeing it. Shakespeare. *Much Ado About Nothing.* Blah blah blah, says Beatrice. Blah blah blah, says Benedick. Your lips are like worms.

"Nice party?" Chilly says.

"Fine." I try to make my voice flatter than a robot's in the hope that he'll leave me alone. No such luck.

"Did you hook up?"

"You have sex on the brain," I say.

"I have sex other places, too."

"I don't think you have sex anywhere, and that's why you have to live vicariously through the rest of us," I say.

"Vicariously," he says. "V-I-C-A-R-I-O-U-S-L-Y. Is that one of the words in your SAT practice book? I bet you use flash cards."

"Is there a reason you always have to sit near me? Isn't there anyone else you can irritate around here?"

"You're my favorite."

He props his chin in his hands and bats his nuclear-accident eyes. Chilly would probably be nice to look at if he wasn't such a jerk, but the jerkiness overwhelms every other thing, the jerkiness is like a great cloud of nerve gas that causes the eyes to roll and the knees to buckle and disgust to claw at the back of the throat. When he first came to our school from Los Angeles in the middle of sophomore year, the girls took notice. Tall, lanky, skin like coffee ice cream, those freaky blue-green eyes, a movie-star strut—what's not to like? I liked it, I'm embarrassed to admit. Oh, he started out great. Notes and gifts and all this attention that I'd never had from anyone. My mom called him "charming." But then Chilly started feeling more comfortable. He started opening his big stupid mouth. He took all the same honors classes that I did, but while I did hours of homework and studied every night, he seemed content to do the least amount possible. He almost never had a book with him. At least not one that he was supposed to. He made fun of me for my study habits, my friends, and my work on the sets of the school plays. He said that the only thing worth my time was him. I finally told him that if he wanted a pet, he should go out and get a poodle.

He's never forgiven me for it.

Today he's got some Japanese comic book that you read backwards. Not that he's opened it yet, because he's too intent on pissing me off. Sometimes he sat near

Kimberly Wong and made her so nervous that she would forget which math problem she was on. And sometimes it was Renee Ostrom, sure to be voted most likely to become a starving artist, who would whip out a piece of paper and draw a quick sketch of Chilly with arrows sticking through his head, or a knife in his heart, or his face shattered in Picasso-like pieces.

Chilly spends about five minutes trying to provoke me when the bell rings. I'm glad that we're not allowed to talk in Mrs. Sayers's study period, and the room is silent except for the scratchy whisper of pages turning. We all hear Cindy Terlizzi's phone when it starts to vibrate. In unison, everyone says, "Phone!"

"Miss Terlizzi," says Mrs. Sayers, who is shelving books in her persnickety way. The edge of every book touches the front of the shelf. "You know that phone is supposed to be turned off when you arrive at school."

"Whatever," says Cindy Terlizzi. When Mrs. Sayers gives her a look, she says, "I know."

"Well then, turn it off," Mrs. Sayers snaps. She picks up the end of her long scarf and flings it around her neck, waiting for satisfaction.

Cindy digs around in her purse for the phone and flips it open with a flick of her wrist. She presses a few buttons and the phone chirps like a sick bird. We all know she's probably getting a text message and is counting on the fact that Mrs. Sayers's own phones are of the rotary or perhaps even the tin can variety.

"Off!" says Mrs. Sayers.

"That's what I'm doing," Cindy says, tsk-tsking, like Mrs. Sayers is just old and grumpy and wrinkled and can't understand modern communication devices. She glances back at the phone in her palm as if she can't quite believe the message she's reading and slaps her hand over her mouth. Then she looks up. Finds me. Smiles.

She's too busy smiling to pay attention to Mrs. Sayers, who, I have to say, is ferret-fast when she wants to be. She swoops down on Cindy, scarf flying like an aviator's, and snatches the phone. "What a clever little gadget," she says.

"Hey!" says Cindy. "Give that back!"

Mrs. Sayers peers down, one eyebrow rucked up. She starts punching random buttons and the phone whirrs. "Very nice," she says, passing it back to Cindy.

Cindy scowls. "You erased it!"

Mrs. Sayers says, "Oh, my! Did I? I'm so very sorry. I hope it wasn't important."

Behind Mrs. Sayers's back, Cindy sticks out her tongue but says nothing. Mrs. Sayers glances my way and I know that whatever was on Cindy's phone was about me—probably about the party, about Pam, about Luke. Well, they could have him. They could all get in line.

Of course, Chilly doesn't miss any of it. He's turning

from Cindy to Mrs. Sayers to me, me to Mrs. Sayers to Cindy. He opens his mouth to say something icky and nuclear and obnoxious, but I cut him off: "Speak and you die."

Chilly gives me his signature "Who, me?" look and opens his mouth again when Mrs. Sayers says, "Yes, Mr. Chillman, please do spare us all. I can't promise you death, but I can promise detention, which I've been told is a bit like dying very, very slowly."

Everybody goes back to not reading, not studying, and not thinking, except for me and a couple of other geeks who think grades are important. At first I can't concentrate, but as the minutes tick by I settle into it, settle into me again: the me who thinks about grade point averages and college applications and various possible futures. I consult my assignment notebook and measure how many days till the final draft of my *Much Ado About Nothing* paper is due, worry about my history test, calculate how many hours I'll have to study for the next calculus exam. It's soothing, the measurements and the calculations and even the worry. Luke is still there, of course, in the back of my head, doing some sort of jock dance of the veils, but I know that he'll fade eventually, taking all his hot boy voodoo into the past.

Finally the bell rings and I'm free of Chilly the Soul Chiller and Cindy Terlizzi, Demon Queen of Text Messaging. As I'm running to my next class, Pete

Flanagan, one of football players, blocks my path.

"Hey, Audrey," he says. His expression is weird, smirky and knowing, which is kind of funny, because Pete really is a rockhead and knows so very little.

"Hi, Pete," I say. I sidestep to go around him, but he moves with me. I notice that there's a bunch of rockheads piling up behind him, all with the same smirky yet stupid expressions, like a bunch of monkeys who've just figured out where all the bananas are.

"Want to go out sometime?" he says.

"What?"

"Go out. Come on, you and me." He jerks a thumb to his friends. "Well, you, me, and some of my boys."

I'm at a loss. This kind of thing hasn't happened in a while. When we were freshmen, clique warfare was rampant. It was considered necessary and maybe even fun to seek out and terrorize everyone who was not exactly like you in the school. I thought most of us, even the football players, had grown out of that. Guess not.

"Sure, guys," I say. "Anytime."

They all let out a whoop as I push past them. Morons.

I motor toward the gym. Out of the corner of my eye I see a finger pointing my way and hear someone laughing, but when I turn, all I see is a row of backs. I start to get a weird feeling, of the weight of eyes, of newly focused attention. In gym, as me and Joelle are pretending to concentrate on the basketball drills, Jeremy Braverman, who has said all of three sentences in three years, says, "I love how you dribble those *balls*, Audrey," over and over again, until Joelle gets shrieky and hysterical and beans him in the head with one of them. I get a note in French class: *"Sur vos genoux!" On your knees!* I turn around to see who wrote it, but no one will meet my eyes. The French in my book blurs into incoherent babble. Did Luke blab to his stupid friends? Did he tell them what we did? No. No! He never talks about his hookups. *Don't ask, don't tell,* he'd say. That was always his deal. So what was going on?

By lunch I can't take the snickering and the weirdness. I make Ash take us to the McDonald's just to get out of the school. "I think someone's spreading rumors about me. I'm getting all these looks. It's making me crazy."

Ash steers the car around to the drive-through window and orders us fries and Cokes. "Really? I haven't heard anything," she says. "Maybe Pam Markovitz is shooting her mouth off. You know what she's like. And she was so jealous of you at the party on Saturday. Pathetic."

"What should I do?" I say.

"Oh, who cares about a bunch of ho's and dumbheads?" Ash tells me. "They'll be babbling about something else by sixth period." Because I forgot to bring cash, she pays for the fries and Cokes and pulls out of the parking lot.

Just as I'm about to open the white bag, my own cell phone buzzes and I scratch around the floor for it. I flip open the phone and check the screen. "Picture mail," I say.

"Maybe Joelle is sending some of the shots she took at the party," says Ash, smashing a fry into her mouth. "I don't know why she bothers. They always suck."

An image pops up and I scroll down to see it. At first I don't understand what it is. And then my insides turn to ice.

"Ash," I say.

"What?"

"Someone took a picture of me."

"Yeah, so?" She looks down at the phone, frowns. "What is it?"

"It's me, Ash. Me and Luke. We were . . ." I trail off, staring at the screen. Luke's head is cut off, but the pale skin of his chest and hips glows in the dark, and his hands clutch fistfuls of the bedspread. Between his knees, a cascade of waist-length blond hair striped with black.

Ash pulls the car over to the side of the road and slams on the brakes. She grabs the phone. "Oh, God," she says. "Who took this?"

"I don't know."

"Where were you?"

"Upstairs in one of the bedrooms."

"Audrey, why didn't you close the freaking door?"

"We did!" I say. "Someone must have seen us go in. Someone must have opened it."

"You didn't hear anyone? You didn't see anything?"

I try to think. The music was so loud—you could hear it coming through the open windows—and then there was the noise that Luke was making. "No," I say. "I didn't hear anything. And I had my eyes closed. I guess Luke did, too."

"*Schweinhund*," she says. "Do you think he planned this?"

"Who?"

"Luke!"

"What? No, I . . ." My head is shaking no no no, but I'm not controlling my own muscles.

And then it hits me all at once. Cindy Terlizzi's slow smile in study. The pointing in the hallways. Pete and the rockheads. Jeremy Braverman, braver than he'd ever been before. "Ash, it's the picture." My stomach does liquid flips and I thrust the fries from my lap. "Someone's been sending around this picture."

The Gauntlet

The parking lot of the school. I don't want to get out of the car.

"Look," says Ash, "let's skip the rest of the day. I don't care if we get in trouble. We can hit the movies or something."

Movies? I can't think, I can't concentrate. I can't understand this. Who took this picture? Who sent it? The return-mail address on the message meant nothing to me. Ash says we can trace it, but I say, Who are we? The freaking FBI?

The phone is still open on my lap. Everyone who gets this picture will know it's me. No one else has hair like this. I wish I'd hacked it off long ago, but I didn't because it was the only thing that made me special. Real special, now. My stomach is locked down so tight that I can't even throw up.

"Say something," Ash says.

This is my private thing, and now it's porn. I feel like someone stole my diary and read it out loud over the speakers. Except that I don't keep diaries. I don't even have a blog. "What am I going to do?"

She doesn't answer, just takes my hand and squeezes it. I would cry if I had any moisture in my body. My throat is dry and scratchy, my tongue a dustrag.

"So do you want to cut for the rest of the day?" Ash asks me.

I want to cut for the rest of the day, the rest of the week, the rest of the year. I want to cut till I go to college. But I have a history test in the afternoon, and if I cut, I'll miss it. The history test was important before, but now it seems like the most important thing in the world. I have to take that test. I have to *ace* that test. It's the only thing I can do.

"No," I say. "I've got a test."

"Audrey, come on—"

"No," I say again. "If I cut today, it will be worse tomorrow."

"Okay," she says. "I'll walk you to your locker."

We get out of the car and walk to the back doors, the doors to the senior wing. The sun has stopped shining, but the air still feels oddly warm and heavy and damp. I'm slogging through molasses, or through dense foliage in some hot, stinking jungle. We push open the doors and immediately the eyes are on me again, the hands hiding wide, smirky grins. It must be all over the school, the bits and codes and ones and zeros flying from one phone to the next, assembling themselves into skin and hair, hands and knees. A hundred blondes between two hundred legs. Me. And me and me, and on and on.

The people part before us and line up on either side of the hallways to watch us go. I hear someone murmur something, and Ash's head whips around. "Shut up, *Arschloch*," she hisses.

We get to my locker and I go through the motions of getting my books. Calc, English, history. We are doing the Constitution in history class, and I run through the amendments in my head. First, free speech and freedom of the press; second, the right to bear arms; third, the right of a property owner to keep soldiers out of his home; fourth, the right of the people to be secure against unreasonable searches and seizures. Unreasonable seizures. Is this a seizure? It feels like one. Someone has ripped my skin off, and all my arteries are hanging out. I can only imagine what they're thinking, what they're saying. *Her? Man, who knew the honors chicks were so easy?*

There's a collective hiss from the crowd in the hall. I hear "Luke! You didn't answer your phone, dude. You have to check this out."

I don't want to look, but I can't stop myself. I turn and see Luke surrounded by a clot of guys, one of them brandishing a phone.

"What is it?" Luke says. He takes a long, lazy pull on the milkshake he must have bought at lunch.

"Just look at it!"

Luke shrugs and takes the phone. One of the rockheads points at the picture helpfully. "This has got to be Audrey Porter," the rockhead says. He says it loudly and clearly. He doesn't care if I'm ten feet away. He doesn't care if I hear.

Luke suddenly stops walking, and the rockhead rams into him. Luke blinks at the picture, his brows beetling as if he's annoyed. Then he thrusts the phone back at the rockhead. "You don't know who that is."

"Come on! That's Porter. Gotta be. Is that you with her?"

Luke walks quickly down the hall toward me. He's not looking at me and Ash at all. His eyes are trained straight ahead, at the doors at the end of the hallway. "You can't see their faces," he says. "That could be any-one."

"No way," says the rockhead. As the group passes by, he jerks his head toward me. "Look at the hair."

"Whatever," Luke says. He doesn't turn my way, just keeps walking. He flicks a hand at the phone. "You guys can find way better stuff on the Internet, if that's what you need." The group floats down the hallway, around the corner and out of sight. I can still hear the gurgling sound of Luke's straw as he polishes off his milkshake.

Pam Markovitz saunters over, with Cindy Terlizzi bringing up the rear like an overeager Maltese. Ash tenses up, waiting for one of them to say something, anything, so that she has an excuse to cut them down. But Pam tips her head, sucks on one of her incisors, and smiles with her kitty-cat teeth. "That was cold. Kind of makes you wish you were a lesbian, doesn't it?"

Oh, yeah, I wish I were a lesbian. An away-in-the-closet, never-had-sex, never-admit-it-to-myself lesbian. Instead, I'm me in calculus, where we are doing limits and continuity. One must be able to calculate limits for the integers x and y. Ms. Iacuzzo's drone could put a coke fiend to sleep, but our calc book is enthusiastic. It has exclamation points. Pick values for x and y! Guess what you think the limits might be!

Test your conjecture by changing the values! The book says calculus is fun! And! Useful! It is useful today, to the uncloseted unlesbian. I'm so busy picking values and testing my conjectures that I can't think about who took a picture of me going down on Luke at Joelle's party; I can't think about Luke himself, his lips so warm when he kissed me and his face flat and frozen when he passed me in the hallway. x is 2 and y is 3. x is 19 and y is 40. x is -435 and y is zero.

In English, Mr. Lambright hands back the first drafts of our *Much Ado About Nothing* papers and there is much ado when the people see all the red marks tattooed on them. *No fair! I can't even read your handwriting! I worked for two weeks on this draft!* Ron Moran, our probable valedictorian, sits smugly at his desk, looking out the window, his paper branded with the customary "EXCELLENT!" Mr. Lambright likes my ideas but thinks I need to work on smoother transitions, I need to link this thought to that thought, one foot in front of the other, like when I walk down the hallway from English to history and I see the faces staring and the mouths snickering and Pete Flanagan shaking his hips and slooooooowly unzipping his fly.

History class. I sit in the back of the room, but I've forgotten about Chilly sitting right next to me. See Chilly snicker. See Chilly stare. See Chilly clap his hands to his cheeks in pretend shock. Hear Chilly say, "Who knew you were such a ho?"

I know what I should say: *With anyone but you.* But I can't bring myself to do it, my mouth is too dry. I don't look at him or look at anyone else; I focus on the amendments, one, two, three, four, five. I sing the Preamble in my head, the way it was sung on the old Schoolhouse Rock CDs my parents bought me when I was a kid. *"We the people, in order to form a more perfect union, establish justice, insure domestic tranquility-e-e-e."* After the bell rings and Mr. Gulliver passes out the tests, I start scribbling. The answers come hot and fast, filling my head. I write until my hand cramps, till the bell rings.

Chilly says, "Ho, ho, ho!"

Chilly says, "Saved by the bell."

Chilly says, "Girls gone wild!"

Chilly says, "Oh my goodness! What will your parents do when they find out?"

I fling my test on Mr. Gulliver's desk and run.

I don't wait for Ash. This little piggy runs all the way home, the whole mile, pack banging into my back with every step. I know what I'll find when I open the door: my mom, sitting at the kitchen table, laptop in front of her, staring off into space or staring into the screen.

But this is not what I find. I open the door and my mom is standing by the kitchen sink, frowning into it.

I should say something. I say, "Hey."

"Look at this," she says, pointing down. "Is that a cricket? Or a grasshopper?"

I look down. Brown bug, big eyes, long legs made for jumping. "Why doesn't it jump out of the sink? Why is it just sitting there?"

"I don't know," my mom says. "It's dumb?"

"Maybe it's dead."

"Poor bug. We'll leave it in peace for a while. A little monument to nature." She pats me on the head—I'm taller, but she still pats—and opens the fridge. She pulls out a Fresca. She lives on Fresca. Grapefruit soda with no calories. I tell her about the carbonation causing bone loss in perimenopausal women (hey, I watch *Dateline NBC*), but she says that since she can't smoke or drink caffeine, what's a little osteoporosis? She tries not to take me too seriously. She tries not to take anything too seriously. She says we have one life and we need to celebrate every day. Her new book, called *Do You Know the Muffin Man?*, is about a cheerful but murderous baker. She's been researching all sorts of muffin recipes and tries them out on us.

She holds out a plate. "Cranberry-orange-oatmeal," she says. "A little gritty, but good."

"No, thanks," I say.

She breaks off a bit of muffin and pops it into her mouth before setting the plate back on the counter. "Are you okay? You look a little peaked."

"I'm fine."

Mom raises her brows but says nothing. She'll wait me out. That's what she does best. Waits. It took her ten years to get a book published, but she never seemed to mind. *I like them,* she'd say. *Maybe someday someone else will like them.* And then someone did. Small publisher, but good enough. Patience is a virtue, she says, but I'm not like her. I can't wait for anything. I'm sixteen, but I'd rather be twenty-six or even thirty-six, free and out in the world, a place where you could sue people for taking pictures of you, a place where people pay for what they do. But then, maybe I am.

She takes her Fresca back to the kitchen table, which is strewn with papers and books and Cat Stevens. "Anything happen at school today?"

I think about my mom's books. No one has ever done more than kiss in any of them, and that was only once. "Not much," I tell her. "I had a test in history. The Constitution, amendments, blah blah blah. I did fine. And I got my draft back from Mr. Lambright."

"Transitions again?" my mom asks.

"What do you think?"

"You never liked transitions, even as a baby. You went from crawling right to running."

"Walking was too slow," I say. "I had places to be." It's an old joke, but this is what we do, so I do it. Her laptop is set to purr every time she gets an e-mail, and it's purring now. She has her own website, Elainepenceporter.com, and her e-mail address is right there for anyone to find. Anyone can write her. Anyone can send her anything. And I know they will. Why wouldn't they?

I sit down at the table. Cat Stevens gently gnaws on my fingers; he loves fingers. I'm not sure if he thinks they're food or what. My mom taps a few keys, scrolls down, taps another key or two.

I wait for the other shoe to drop. Or is it the axe? The knitting needles? The muffins? "Anything interesting?"

"Nah," she says. "Not unless we need a new mortgage or some Viagra."

I try to laugh and instead make a sort of strangled sound. "Is Dad still at the store?" My dad owns a formal-wear shop—wedding gowns, party dresses, that sort of thing.

"When isn't he at the store?" my mom says. "He should be home about seven or seven thirty." Angel is also her store—they opened it together fifteen years ago. She still works there on weekends, and so do I when I don't have too much studying. Dad never leaves. And even when he's not working, he's working.

Her computer purrs again. More mail. Click, click, click. Frown. "What?" she says, more to herself than to me. But of course I know what.

"It's a picture, right?"

She glances up from the computer and considers me in her careful way. She tips the screen so that I can see what's on it. Two striped kittens, with the message "My new babies, Bastet and Vladimir!"

"Oh," I say. "Cute."

"You were expecting something else?"

I should tell her. I want to tell her. I don't know how. What are the words? Mouth? Head? Me? I say, "No."

"No?"

I shrug like I don't know what she's talking about. *Silly mom!*

"Uh-huh. Well. I'm assuming you have a mountain of homework to do, yes?"

"Yeah. I've got to work on those transitions for Mr. Lambright. Otherwise I won't get an A."

"Oh, my!" she says, with mock horror. I sigh, and her expression softens. "It's your senior year. I think you can relax just a little."

"Like you?" I say, pointing at her computer.

"Don't you worry about me, I relax plenty," she says. "It's you I'm concerned about."

"You should worry about Dad," I say. "He's the one with the high blood pressure."

"Which you'll have before you're eighteen. You're just like him." She smiles at me. "Audrey, I think you can start having a little bit of fun. So you don't get an A this once. So you get an A minus. Is that really the worst that could happen to you?"

I can't look at her when I answer. "No. I guess not."

I go up to my room and throw my knapsack on my bed. I feel sort of itchy all over, and I'm not sure what to do with myself. First I go over to the toothpick village. It is what it sounds like it is, a village built out of toothpicks and Popsicle sticks. I've got houses, a couple of churches, stores, roads, a windmill, whatever—all painted and mounted on a slab of wood. I started building it when I was nine, right around the time I got sick of Barbies. Every once in a while, I work on something new. It's a totally twisted, pathetic hobby, I know, but I've always loved building things. It's sort of like meditation, except for, you know, the toothpicks.

But today, the toothpick village isn't cutting it—I can't think of a single thing that I'd want to add, and it seems like nothing more than a kindergartner's art project or a load of firewood. So I sit at my desk. I flick on the computer and the machine hums to life and starts pinging, meaning I've got about four thousand instant messages. I don't even want to read them. I start deleting them, but I can't help but see a few, mostly from IM names I don't recognize:

Instant Message with "sweetyPI567"
Last message received at: 3:42:10 PM

sweetyPI567: U R such a ho! your dad
should call his store Sluts R Us!

Instant Message with **"691uvvver"**
Last message received at: 4:19:36 PM
691uvvver: will u marry me? will u at
least suck me off????

Instant Message with **"ritechuschik2424"**
Last message received at: 6:10:22 PM
ritechuschik2424: u do what u want to do
and don't let any one stop u. its ur
life. U R not a slut ur just trying
to have fun. LDS is HOT!

I've got e-mail, too. A few people helpfully sent me
a copy of the picture, just in case I haven't been humiliated enough. Joelle sends a few ALL-CAPS messages
telling me that Ash told her what happened and claiming that she will personally eviscerate Luke DeSalvio
(unless, of course, I still like him). Then she says that
what I need to do is deny absolutely everything and that
she'll tell everyone she saw Pam Markovitz or Cindy
Terlizzi running around in a blond wig. I erase all the
messages, even the ones from Jo. I keep pressing the
button till there are no more messages in my in-box,
and then I press it a few more times, just to make sure.

My phone rings inside my backpack and I sit there, listening to it buzz. Later, as I'm reworking my paper for Mr. Lambright, it buzzes again. And when I'm doing my calc homework. And again when I'm studying bio. Buzz, buzz, like wasps hitting a window. If they buzz long enough, if they hit hard enough, maybe they'll all die.

"Audrey?" My mother's voice warbles up the stairs. It must be time for dinner—not that I want to eat anything, now or ever. My stomach has shut down, packed up, and left for a vacation. Bye-bye, stomach. It occurs to me that I could actually lose a few pounds by the time I'm ready to eat again, and then I can't believe I'm thinking what I'm thinking. I must be sick. There's plenty of evidence. Once, when I was about eleven, my mom was asking me what kinds of words kids use in place of swearwords when teachers are around, because she had a kid in one of her books and wanted to have him swear without actually swearing. I told her we called people jerks, losers, and dorks. And I told her that sometimes we went all British, calling people prats and gits and saying "bloody hell" with accents that made it sound like "bluddy hill." And then I told her about our very favorite non-swear swearword, one that we recently discovered and said all the time. "What is it?" she said.

"Cocksucker," I told her.

Her jaw dropped open almost to the table, and her eyes popped wide. "Audrey," she said. "That is most definitely a swearword."

"It is?"

"Absolutely, definitely a swearword. You guys have to try and stop saying it, okay?"

By then I was blushing so hard that my cheeks sizzled. How could I have been so dumb to not know a swearword when I heard one?

"Do you know what it means?"

And I'd told her I did—and I did sort of—but I thought it was more like a kiss, and how bad could a kiss be?

I go downstairs, where things are more than bad. They are worse. My mom is sitting at the table, which hasn't been set for dinner. There's no food on the stove, no pizza box by the sink, and nothing roasting in the oven. My dad stands at the kitchen counter, his jacket still on, as if he can't decide if he's coming or going. He pulls a folded piece of paper out of his pocket and smooths it out on the counter. I don't need to see it, but I can't help but see. The picture, again. This time with a message: "Look at Your Little Angel Now."

A Beautiful Thing

*D*ad does not know what to do with himself.

He takes off his jacket and holds it over one arm.

Then he switches it to the other arm. Then he

throws it on the counter. He pulls it from the

counter and hangs it over the back of a chair. As

if there were a person inside, he pats the shoulders

of the jacket. He doesn't look at me.

I am sitting at the kitchen table with my mom, counting the scratches in the wood. There are a lot of scratches. Most of the stuff we have is old or cheap or both. My parents love flea markets and antique stores. Not too long ago, my mom thought about opening her own vintage clothing boutique, until my dad reminded her how much she hated the business end of business.

"Where did this come from?" my mom asks. Not me, my dad.

"Someone sent it to the store e-mail address," he says.

My mom turns to me. "Is this why you seemed so depressed before?"

I nod.

"What happened? Is someone playing a joke on you? Did someone dress up like you?"

For a minute I think about saying, *Yes! A joke! It's just a big joke!* But I shake my head no.

My mom's fingers brush the edge of the paper on the table. "So this *is* you?"

My eyes on the floor, I nod yes.

"From Saturday night?"

More mute nodding.

My dad's hands tighten around the shoulder of the jacket. "Did someone force you to—"

"No, Dad," I say. "Nobody forced me."

"I don't understand," he says. "How could someone

take a picture? Did you let them?"

"No!" I say.

But my dad doesn't stop. "Is that what's going on at parties now?"

"John. . . ," my mom says. "Let her talk."

My dad snatches up the picture. "Who is this?" he says, jabbing a finger at the naked chest floating above my hair.

"Nobody you know," I say.

My dad's jaw quivers like I just smacked him. "Nobody?" he says.

I'm not crying. It's impossible that I'm not, but I'm not. I feel cold and hard, like marble. An Audrey-shaped statue sitting at the kitchen table. Stevie the marmalade catdog jumps in my statue lap and licks my statue fingers. I barely feel his teeth as he nibbles.

My mom's lips are moving, forming words and then biting them back. Finally she says, "Is this your boyfriend?"

I almost laugh, but my marble mouth just isn't that mobile. "Sort of," I say. "Not anymore. I broke up with him."

"Christ!" my dad says. He stares at me. "Tell me that you at least used protection."

"We didn't need protection," I said. "I mean, not for that. I don't think." I can't believe I'm saying it as I'm saying it. This is not embarrassment. It's not humiliation. It's something deeper and darker and more awful, like a giant black hole of spinning saw blades.

He looks like he has a bee caught in his throat. "You don't need . . ."

My mom gives him a warning look and he clamps his mouth shut. She says, "So you were . . . with your boyfriend, and someone took the picture. Do you know who did it?"

"No," I say. "I have no idea. Somebody must have snuck up on us."

My mom nods again as if she understands, but I can tell that she doesn't, that she's completely out of her element, that she's gearing up to call in the professionals. They didn't do this in her day, maybe, or they didn't have the physical evidence. No digital cameras or picture phones. No e-mail or blogs or instant messages. No photographs to send to other people's dads. "Who else has seen this?"

"Everyone."

She winces. "Oh, honey."

My dad says, "What do you mean, *everyone*?" He's frowning so hard and so deeply that his dark eyebrows bunch up in folds over his nose.

"They've been sending it from phone to phone at school. All day today."

There's silence. I don't know how long. We can hear the clock tick. We can hear Stevie's tongue as he patiently sands away my fingerprints.

Then my dad says, "I'll call the phone company."

"Why?"

"To find out who was sending the picture around."

"Can you do that?"

"I can try," he said. His mouth was a thin, tight seam. "I'm sure it's the boy."

"Who?" I said.

He points at the photo. "This one. He probably had some friend take the picture."

I sigh. "I don't think so. He couldn't have known."

"Known what?"

That I would unbutton his shirt and spread it like a curtain. That I would slide his belt from his belt loops and fling it behind me.

But then, maybe he did know. Maybe he and everyone else could guess where it was all going and I was the only one who couldn't.

"Known what?" my dad says again. "He couldn't have known what?"

We used to play a lot of catch when I was little. I can still throw a baseball like a guy and my football pass has a decent, if wobbly, spiral. *Good arm, good arm,* my dad would tell me, grinning. Now my father is staring at me as if he has no idea who I am or where I came from.

"I don't know," I say. "Never mind." My dad whips

his jacket from the back of the chair and stalks out of the room.

"Audrey," my mom says. "He's just upset right now. He'll get over it."

"Sure," I say. "Right."

It's clear my dad is not going to get over anything until he finds someone to sue. Or shoot. We spend Monday night in virtual silence while my dad does endless Google searches on laws regarding the transmission of photos over cell phones. My mom brings me hot tea and more hot tea and spends a lot of time trying to figure out what, exactly, she should say to me. We try to watch a new cop show—my mom loves cop shows and she got me hooked—but the episode is about these boys who date-rape a girl at some exclusive Manhattan high school. Neither me or my mom can take it. We turn it off and go to bed early. I don't sleep.

Tuesday morning and still we're not over it, won't be over it for a long long time. My dad leaves before me so that he doesn't have to look at me. My mom, wearing her usual uniform of sweatpants and a sweatshirt, sits at the kitchen table staring off into space, a cup of coffee cooling in front of her. She looks like I feel. Dark circles, hair puffy and matted. The sun filtering through the cracks in the curtains highlights a web of wrinkles around her eyes.

"Did you sleep?" she asks me.

"Not really," I say.

"Me neither."

She stands, walks to the coffeepot, and pours another cup of coffee. She adds milk and lots of sugar, and hands it to me. I only drink coffee once in a while, but she knows I need it. I grab a yogurt, a napkin, and a spoon and we sit at the kitchen table. We've got two minutes before Ash comes to pick me up.

"I'm so sorry about what happened," she says.

"Me, too."

"I don't understand how someone could have been so cruel. To take that picture of you and send it around. I can't stand it. Who could be that mad at you?"

"It could be someone who doesn't even know me, Mom." I open the lid on the yogurt and take a spoonful. It tastes like glue. "It could be a random person who just thinks it's funny."

"Funny?" my mom says. She turns her mug around and around in her hands. "I want to kill whoever did this."

"You mean you want to kill me."

Her head snaps up. "Of course not!"

"Dad does."

"Stop that," she says. "Your dad loves you."

"He still wants to kill me."

"This is hard for him. For any dad. He doesn't want

54

anyone to take advantage of you." She takes a deep breath. "Sex is a beautiful thing. If it's with the right person. Was this . . . have there . . . been others?"

I don't say anything. I get up, take the container of yo-glue, and go to toss it in the trash. I see that the picture my dad printed at the store has been torn into little pieces and thrown in the garbage, right on top of the cranberry-orange-oatmeal muffins.

"Audrey, I just want you to be careful," my mom says.

I don't say, *Like you were?* There's a honk from outside. "That's Ash," I say. "I have to go."

At school, anyone who hadn't seen the picture has now seen it over and over again. I find a copy of it pasted on my locker. I grab it, crumple it to a ball, and throw it on the floor. I haven't said a word to Ash all the way to school, and she hasn't asked me to, but now I tell her about my parents.

She sucks her breath through her teeth so quickly that she whistles. *"Scheisse,"* she says. "How did they find out?"

"Someone sent the picture to the store. My dad brought a copy home. They thought that it was someone playing a prank."

"How did they take it?"

"My dad's mad. At first he thought someone, um . . ."

I lower my voice. "Someone, you know, forced me or whatever, but I told them that no one forced me to do anything."

"You should have said someone forced you."

"Yeah, right. And have them call the police? I don't think so." I stuff my jacket into my locker. "My dad can't even look at me."

"What about your mom?"

"She's trying, but she doesn't know what to say. It took her till this morning just to say the word 'sex.'"

"Jeez," says Ash.

Cindy Terlizzi and Pam Markovitz walk by. Pam grins at me and gives me the thumbs-up sign.

Ash scowls, then sighs. "It's bad now, I know. Really bad. But people will forget."

"Yeah?" I say. "When?"

"Soon. They always do."

I know they will, someday, but that doesn't help the frozen spot where my guts should be. That doesn't stop the stares and snickers and giggles in the hallway. That doesn't stop Chilly from whispering poison in my ear. That doesn't keep the more girl-impaired of the male honor students from eyeing me with this strange curiosity, like they want to pin me down to a dissecting tray and prod me with sharp instruments. Even Ron "Valedictorian" Moran, who's had a girlfriend for the last year, stares. I stare right back. What was Ron doing with his girlfriend when they thought no one was paying attention, when they thought their parents were out for the afternoon? Ron looks away.

All day, I bury myself in work, in words. I sink into them like a bath. My friends give me my space, but the teachers yammer all around me. Limits, amendments, oxygen cycles, Shakespeare. This is important and that is important and all of it will be on the test. I write, underline, highlight, repeat. I get text messages and delete them. A few people pass me stupid notes that I know say horrible things, and I shove them into my books or backpack without looking at them. At lunch I will go outside and set them all on fire. Ash will throw the ashes out her car window.

"What I really want to know is, Who took that picture?" Ash says. She's taken me to the diner to eat. "Do you really think that Luke had nothing to do with it?"

"I don't know," I say.

Ash scoops up a spoonful of mashed potatoes and gravy, what she orders every time we come to the diner, day or night. Her eyes narrow. "What about Chilly? He's still dogging you like he owns you."

"I don't know," I say.

Ash puts down her spoon. "Don't you want to know who did this? Doesn't this make you mad?"

"Well, yeah," I tell her.

"Well, yeah?" she says. "I'd be furious! I'd want to

kill someone! You got more upset that time Madame Kellogg gave you a B plus on your French report."

"I just wish it never happened," I say. "I wish I'd never done it."

She tucks a stray curl behind her ear and sighs. "You love him, right?"

That seems funny to me. I love my parents. I love Ash and Joelle. I love my cat. Luke is—was—a different story. Luke is like a creature from another planet. Can you ever really love a creature from another planet? Someone who could jump on his spaceship and rocket off to Pluto at any minute? "I don't know."

Ash is getting annoyed with all that I don't know. "Yes, you did. Isn't that why you were all weirded out with the friends-with-benefits thing? Weren't you jealous of all those other girls? Didn't you want to go out with him?" She eats another spoonful of mashed potatoes.

I want to tell her the whole story. I *should* tell her. She's my best friend and I need her to understand. But I'm not sure if she will. After Jimmy, I'm not sure if she can. So I agree with her. Yes, I was weirded out. Yes, I was jealous. I don't know what else I was—insane? obsessed?—but I think if I say "I don't know" one more time, she'll kill me.

Luckily, or unluckily, she decides to let me live. Sixth period, and I've gotten through most of my classes and even managed to eat two bites of Ash's potatoes at lunch. Even though I've got my eyes pinned to the floor, I see Luke walking down the hallway as I'm trying to get to history. It's not the blond hair that catches me, it's the movement—the rolling, easy walk, the walk that says he could run very very fast if there were ever any need to. He's alone this time, no gaggle of rockheads shoving phones at him. Then he sees me. He never said much more than "hey" to me in public before, but this is a new low. His face stiffens and his eyes narrow, and his lip curls up as if he's disgusted, as if he can't even bear to look. He speeds up, passes me, and keeps on rolling, like a wave that jumps the beach and takes you out at the knees.

Once More, with Feeling

The first time was Ash's party, a back-to-school barbecue without any of the actual barbecuing. There must have been a shortage of parties that weekend, because the entire senior class showed up to mourn the end of the summer. Ash's parents had taken her little brother out of town, stupidly trusting Ash not to do anything stupid (like, say, throw a party for the entire senior class). But there we were, in Ash's house, with everyone packed inside and spilling outside, a blur of cutoffs and halter tops and precancerous brown skin, all of us hugging our friends and hugging total strangers and loving the world. Even Chilly seemed less Chilly somehow—less obnoxious, less angry—maybe because there were chicks there who'd never met him before and were willing to give him a shot. I remember looking out the open window to the backyard and seeing a girl run by wearing only her underwear, but moving too fast for me to see her face. I could hear her, though. She was giggling like a maniac.

Once in a while, Ash would announce that the drunk and otherwise hammered would have their keys and maybe even their cars confiscated to guard against possible injuries and subsequent lawsuits (her dad is a lawyer), but as these things go, the party was tame. Something was in the air, some late-August-evening magic-fairy nice dust that made us all mostly friendly and sort of giddy and not too destructive. It seemed that we all understood that this was our last summer together, that next year at this time most of us would already be gone—off to start the rest of our lives.

Even I wasn't exactly me. School hadn't started yet, and I had nothing in particular to hyperventilate over. I'd already taken all my entrance exams, and my college applications weren't due for months. I felt so strange—untethered from myself, like I was watching myself from a distance. Like I was my own shadow.

It felt kind of good. A relief.

Being me is tiring.

The only problem was the late arrival of Jimmy and his ho girlfriend. I guess he figured that since he and Ash had broken up six months before and there wasn't another party in the whole town, he could show up and blend in without getting Ash too crazy. Right. Like Jimmy could blend in anywhere with a chick named *Cherry*, the very same chick that he dumped Ash for. Since they'd broken up, Ash had serious radar for Jimmy. I think she could spot him a mile away. She could sense him. She could *smell* him.

So when he showed up with Cherry on his arm and tried to mingle, Ash cornered them in the kitchen, screamed at him, told him what a loser he was, how much she hated him and how he needed to take his slut out of her house. A normal person would have gotten all embarrassed, but not Jimmy.

"Listen, Ashley," he said, drawing out the "sh" sound as if he were singing a lullaby.

"Ash!" said Ash. "The name's *Ash*."

"Ash," he said. "Look, I'm sorry about everything. I never meant to hurt you. Never." He brushed his long rocker hair out of his enormous brown eyes. Jimmy has cocker-spaniel eyes, eyes that could get you to believe almost anything he says. "I'm really, really sorry. How many times can I say it?"

"You can say it again, you *Arsch*! And then you can get out of my house!"

Jimmy nodded, tipping his head as if digesting her words. "I hear you. But it's been a long time now. Don't you think we all need to move on?"

Cherry slid her arms around Jimmy's waist and looked at Ash. "I hope that we can be friends." Then she reached up and yanked at her bra strap, maximizing all visible cleavage.

Ash spat a vast array of truly inventive swearwords in several languages. I thought she was going to gut Jimmy with a steak knife or rip out Cherry's throat with her teeth, so I tried to drag her from the room while giving Jimmy my fiercest best-friend evil eye.

I was still trying to convince Ash to come with me and cool off when I saw Luke DeSalvio peek into the room and then double back. "Whoa! Rumble!" he said, but nobody listened; Ash was too busy screaming, Jimmy too busy looking sad and soulful. Luke's eyes went from Jimmy to Cherry to Ash to me to Jimmy again, until he pulled Jimmy and Cherry into the dining room. We couldn't hear what else Luke said, but we could see them through the doorway: Jimmy nodding, glancing at Ash, looking at the floor, nodding again.

Finally, Jimmy came back and mumbled something like, "Sorrynevermeanttohurtyouwe'releavingbye." Then he grabbed Cherry by the elbow and steered her out the door and out of the house.

Ash gaped at Luke. "What did you say to him?"

Luke shrugged. "I told him he was being a tool."

"That's all?" Ash said.

Luke's mouth turned up at the corners. "I might have said a few other things. Like, this is your house and if you didn't want him here he had to get out. He *was* being a tool, right?"

"Among other things," said Ash.

"And this *is* your house, right?"

"Yeah."

"Okay, then."

"Okay," Ash said, bewildered by this show of gallantry from the Jock King, someone we had admired from afar but never had much reason to talk to. "Thanks."

"No problem," Luke said. He paused. "You're not going to be all depressed now, are you?"

Ash said, "Excuse me?"

"You're not going to throw us all out so that you can drown yourself in your bathtub, right?"

"Don't worry. The party must go on." Ash tossed her curly hair. "I might fling myself out the second-floor window, but I'll wait till everyone's gone home."

"Great to hear it," he said.

"And not because I'm depressed; because I'm really really really pissed off."

"Even better. You're beautiful when you're angry."

Ash raised her eyebrow, the one that she had just gotten pierced a few days before. "I'm beautiful all the time."

Luke laughed. "Is that the only piercing you have?"

"Maybe."

"And do you have a tattoo to go with it?"

"Maybe."

"Where?"

"Like I'd tell you."

I thought I was witnessing this amazing thing. He wasn't her usual type—she normally went for the tall, dark, and smoldering, and not the medium-sized, sunny, and golden—but he was hot by anybody's standards. If anyone could take Jimmy off her mind, it would be Luke. He didn't seem like a bad guy, not after he got Jimmy to leave. Plus, he had the most incredible hands I'd ever seen. Man hands. Big, long-fingered.

He turned to me. "Hi."

"Hi," I said.

"You're Audrey."

"You're Luke."

"You know, one of my friends thinks that your hair is fake."

"Her hair isn't fake!" said Ash.

"I didn't say it was what *I* thought, I said it was what one of my *friends* thought. He doesn't think hair could grow that long. That you must be wearing those extension things."

"Your friend's a bonehead," I said.

"Yeah," said Ash.

I was so busy getting my head around the fact that Luke DeSalvio and one of his friends had discussed my hair that it took me a second to notice that Luke had lifted a lock and was rubbing the ends between his fingers. He looked directly into my eyes, so that I could see his had rings of dark blue around rings of light. "Feels real enough," he said. He dropped the lock, smoothing it back over my shoulder. "I'll have to go tell my friend."

"So go," Ash told him.

But he didn't. He hung out with me and Ash in the kitchen, making stupid jokes about googly-eyed guitar guys, about Big Boobs Barbie, and about hair extensions till he got Ash to laugh out loud. After a while, his friend Nardo ambled in, wondering where Luke had disappeared to and who with. Nardo was a jock, too, an odd one, one who played sax for the school jazz band. He was also on the track team, where he got a lot of attention for jumping as far as he possibly could.

The four of us ended up sitting at the kitchen table, playing blackjack with a deck of cards Ash scrounged up. Luke foraged for alcohol and found beer for himself and Nardo and some kind of hard lemonade stuff for me and Ash from God knows where. I hate cards and I don't like my lemonade spiked with anything but sugar, but I don't remember any of it being that much fun before, with the drinks fuzzing my vision around the edges and Luke's hand brushing my hair and my arm. I thought Ash would be mad that he'd sat next to me instead of her, but she didn't seem to mind it at all. Nardo was really cute, all long arms and legs, with a smile that opened up his whole face.

At some point the game got so stupid we weren't really playing, and Nardo got busy inspecting Ash's eyebrow ring up close, so I grabbed up the cards and started to build a house with them. Watching Nardo prod Ash's still-raw eyebrow with his pinky made me nervous—it seemed so personal, digging around in someone's fresh, if self-inflicted, wound. I tried to concentrate on the card house, but Luke was watching me. That made me nervous, too.

"Was it him?" I blurted, pointing at Nardo. When I was nervous, I blurted.

"Him what?" Luke said.

"Yeah, me what?" Nardo said. He had one hand on Ash's forehead, as if he were checking if she had a fever.

"Luke said that one of his friends thought my hair was fake. Was it you?" I said.

"Oh, that," said Nardo. "He must not have heard me right. I was telling him that *my* hair was fake." He dipped his head toward Ash. "Feel it."

Ash ran her hand through Nardo's short, dark hair. "Totally fake. What is that? Nylon?"

"Polyester," said Nardo.

"What happened to your real hair?" Ash said.

"Lost in a bizarre weed-whacking incident," Nardo said. Then he leaned in and kissed Ash. She stared at him cross-eyed for a split second, then kissed back.

"Don't watch the mating animals," said Luke. "They could get violent." He handed me another card and gave me a drumroll on the seat of his chair while I balanced the card on top of the others.

But Ash and Nardo kept kissing, not caring that me and Luke were sitting right there. When Nardo pulled Ash onto his lap, Luke said, "I think that's our cue."

We left Ash and Nardo making out in the kitchen. It was late, really late, because most of the people had gone home and the few that were left were crashing all over the place. Underwear girl turned out to be Joelle, who was sleeping on one of the couches in her hot-pink bra and red shorts. I should have known. Joelle has a killer body that her personal trainer works very hard to achieve, and she's never afraid to show it off. She says that an actor has to be ready to use every asset at her disposal.

Luke whistled at her, but she didn't wake up.

"Impressive," he said. "You guys are pretty good friends, right?"

"Yeah." Normally, I would have been self-conscious about my own non-personal-trainer–enhanced body. My own assets include boobs that could be bigger, a butt that could be smaller, and abs that could be flatter. But then, at that party, I had a weird and totally uncharacteristic thought: *Oh, well, nothing you can do about it now.* The breeze whipping through the open windows smelled a little like flowers, a little like grass, a little like rain. Everything that usually worried me seemed far away and not very important.

"Joelle and I met doing the plays. I'm not *in* the plays, though. I design the sets and stuff."

Luke smiled. "You act like I don't know who you are. I know who you are."

For some reason that made me blush.

"You want to go outside for a while?" he said.

Some tiny part of me—the shadow part, the part that watched—shouted, *Outside? Luke Freaking DeSalvio is asking you OUTSIDE? Is this a joke? What does it MEAN? What's he DOING? What will you SAY?*

I said, "Sure. Let's go outside."

He opened the screen door and we stepped out onto the grass. Ash has a huge yard with a fence all around it, plus an enormous wooden swing set for her little brother, Bo.

"Sweet," Luke said. "How about I swing you?"

"No, thanks."

"You think I'm not strong enough?"

Before I had a second to swallow it back, I said, "Show me what you got, big man."

He pulled back the sleeve of his T-shirt and made a muscle for me. Not too big, not too small. I squeezed it, feeling like the teenage Goldilocks. The skin on the underside of his arm was surprisingly soft, smooth as my own cheek. I asked him to show me the other arm. Just to make sure he was up for the task, I added.

"Oh, I'm up for a lot of things," Luke said, which made me giggle idiotically.

We went over to the swing set and I sat down on one of the swings. While I launched with my feet, he gave me a small push.

"Come on, then," I said, my fake English accent making it safer to tease. "You can do better than that."

He grabbed ahold of both ends of the seat, but instead of pushing, he walked backwards until I was nearly facing the ground, nearly slipping off. Then he let go. When I swung back again, I felt the heat of his palms on the small of my back, where my shirt rode up. I leaned into them and thrust my legs straight into the sky, and then fell down through the air into his hands, catch and release, catch and release. Everything—the party, Luke, the whole night—seemed impossible and ridiculous, and most likely a lemonade-induced hallucination. I got to thinking I could do anything: sing, dance, fly. I decided to jump the way I used to when I was a kid. I felt Luke's palms on my back and then the swift climb through the air. At the last minute, I shot off the swing. For one wonderful second I soared like a crazy bird, but then I dropped, landing funny and falling over sideways. I wasn't hurt, but I wondered how stupid it must have looked.

It was not the kind of night for dwelling, though. I was too giddy for that. Instead of getting to my feet, I rolled over to look up at the stars.

"Are you all right?" Luke asked, sinking to his knees beside me.

"I'm fine."

"What are you doing?"

I heard myself say, "I felt like being horizontal."

Luke plopped down next to me, our shoulders touching. I felt my skin scorching the grass beneath me.

"Do you know the names of any of the stars?" he asked.

"No," I said.

"You don't? I thought you were some kind of genius."

"Do *you* know any of the names?"

"Let me see," he said, pointing up at the sky. "Okay. Right there. That's the South Star."

"You mean the North Star?"

"No, I mean the South Star. And that's the Big Dogpile. And that's the Little Dipshit."

It was dumb, but I laughed anyway. As I laughed, he grabbed one of my hands, twining his fingers in mine. He raised himself up on one elbow to look at me. I could almost feel the muscles in my eyes working to make my pupils bigger, so that I could take him all in.

His fingers tightened. "You're a good card player."

Out popped "I'm good at a lot of things."

"And that's good to know." Suddenly he was kissing me. He was soft and slow at first, nibbling and searching to the point where I wanted to grab him by the ears and make him kiss me like he meant it, already. And then he did, all hungry, as if the inside of my mouth and the whole of my tongue were made of strawberries or ice cream or something equally sweet and delicious. My head swam and I was grateful that I was already lying down. If I'd been standing, I'd have swooned like a character from a Victorian novel.

After a while, he pulled away and touched my lips with his fingers. "What are you smiling at?"

"I'm smiling?" I said.

"You're smiling."

The late-August-evening magic-fairy nice dust made it easy to be honest. "I like kissing with the Little Dipshit shining down on us. Twinkle, twinkle."

He laughed, a short bark of surprise. "You're sort of a weird girl, aren't you?"

"So?"

"So," he said. He gathered a handful of my hair and brought it to his nose. "Princess hair," he murmured. "Smells like honey." He combed through it with his fingers, twirling and twisting the strands. Then he pressed his lips to my ear. "You like the whole kissing thing, huh?"

I dared to slide my hand up the underside of his arm, to feel that soft skin. "Yes."

"What's that saying that actors have when they rehearse a scene? Something about doing it again with emotion, or whatever?"

I thought a minute. "'Once more, with feeling'?"

"That's it," he said. In one smooth motion he was on top of me, settling in like a puzzle piece. He kissed me again with so much feeling it would have brought a dead girl back to life.

I Am Hamlet

It's Wednesday after school at the Drama Club. I am trying to keep my mind blank by repeating the word "black" over and over again in my head. It doesn't work. People are surprised to see me sitting in the auditorium like it was any other day. I get some smirks from some of the freshmen and sophomores who don't really know me, but my friends say things like "Um!" "Oh!" "Hey!" or "Hi!" "Umohheyhi": Native American for *"How the hell can* you *show your face in public*????"

To me, the auditorium isn't public, it's like home. A huge, echoey home with squeaky old seats that are about as comfortable as lava rock and a moth-eaten blue velvet curtain pulled back to expose the naked, strangely sad-looking stage. There's a small stack of papers sitting right at the edge. People point to the stack of papers and whisper to one another, but no one moves to take a peek.

Joelle sits in the seat next to me. Her eyes are red from crying. For me. "Dirtbags," she whispers.

"Who?" I say.

"The dirtbags who took that picture," she says. "Of *my* friend. At *my* party. If I ever find out who did it, I. Will. Kill. Them. I will personally shove my purple boot down their throats." She extends one of her long legs and displays the purple suede boot, which has a four-inch spike heel a drag queen would envy. If it were anyone else talking, anyone else crying, I would think it's an act. But this is Joelle. She means everything she says. At least at the moment she says it.

A geeky little freshman with carroty hair glances back at us. "What are you looking at?" Joelle snaps. She pokes me in the arm. "I wonder which of these skinny children are here to try out for the play? I'm sure we're doing *Antigone*. Ms. Godwin does *Antigone* every four years. I don't have to tell you that the part belongs to me. No one here can do a better Antigone, I don't care what color their hair is!"

"You're right about that," I say. I'm not here for the tryouts, I just want to know what play we're doing so that I can think about the set. I've worked on every set since I was thirteen years old and too shy to audition for a part. Sometimes I have a big job, and sometimes it's a small one. Today I'm hoping for an opera set in medieval Venice so that I'm forced to figure out how to build a bunch of working canals, so that I don't have a single brain cell free to think about anything else. Not one synapse firing off a teeny tiny replica of a blow job over and over again. Not one stray neuron pulsing about Luke DeSalvio and how he's a hero and I'm a whore.

Joelle reaches into her bag and pulls out a list. "Here are some more names I came up with." Joelle's last name is Lipshitz, which, she says, is unacceptable for a human being, let alone an actress. She's been trying to come up with something glam and different, something she will adopt when she gets out of high school and runs off to New York City to become famous (or when her dad drives her to and from the city to become famous).

I look at the paper. She's written:

Joelle Paris
Joelle Roma
Joelle Asia

Joelle Nepal
Joelle Geneva
Joelle St. Petersburg
Joelle Quebec

"What do you think?" she says.

"I'm sensing a theme," I tell her.

"Any favorites?"

"You forgot Joelle Boise. Or Joelle Long Island."

She whips the paper from my hand. "You are totally too traumatized to take me seriously right now. I swear I'm going to kill whoever did this to you. I'm going to shove this boot down their throats."

"You already said that."

"Then I'm going to run them over with my car."

"You mean your dad's car."

The carroty redhead in front of us risks another glance, and Joelle shrieks, "You, too, if you don't stop staring at my friend! She is not a zoo exhibit!"

Of course, everyone turns around and stares at me as if I were a zoo exhibit. Joelle tells them all to STOP STARING!! JUST STOP!! Just then the side door swings open and Ms. Godwin marches into the auditorium. Ms. Godwin is aptly named, tall as a goddess, with a low oboe voice that sounds as if she's talking through a tube of wrapping paper. She is wearing what she always wears, a long, flowing top and skirt and sharp-heeled character shoes that snap when she walks.

"What I would like," she says as she moves to stand in front of the stage, "is for you to stop shrieking, Ms. Lipshitz. They can hear you in Sri Lanka."

Everyone settles down—including Joelle—and waits for Ms. Godwin to tell us which play we'll be doing, and thus what our lives will be like for the next two months. But first we have to get through her customary "welcome" speech. I mouth the words with her:

"Hello. I am Victoria Godwin, Ms. Godwin to you. *Ms.*, not Miss, not Mrs., Godwin. For those of you who are new to the school or perhaps new to this program, I am the drama teacher. Which means that I am the queen of this auditorium. What I say goes. You don't have a vote and you don't have influence. When I select someone for a part, it is that person's part. If I select you for the set design team, then the set design team is where you belong. Begging me will not change any of my decisions, nor will flattery, tantrums, gifts, or flowers. You will attend every rehearsal you need to attend. You will perform every task you need to perform. I will not police you, I will not scream at you, I will not call your parents, I will not ask for hall passes, I will not demand proof of your citizenship. Why? Because I don't care. However, if you show up for a rehearsal and you don't know your lines, you're out. If you're on the crew and you don't pull your weight, you're out. If it is your job to place props during rehearsals and we find you behind the curtains making out with your boyfriend instead, then you're out."

Someone giggles, and Ms. Godwin stares stonily. "Have I said something funny?"

The giggles stop.

"Now, I realize that some of you may be expecting your typical high school drama, but I want to do something different this season."

Next to me, Joelle inhales sharply.

"I have a friend, a playwright, who has graciously allowed me to license a wonderful, humorous piece of work based on Shakespeare's *Hamlet*."

"Great," murmurs Joelle. "Ophelia. She's such a wimp. I hate playing wimps."

"The play is called *I Am Hamlet*, and it turns Shakespeare on his angst-y little head. In this play, Hamlet is a woman. Of course, the weight of the play will fall on Hamlet's shoulders. I'm going to need a very strong actress to carry this." Ms. Godwin's eyes briefly flick toward Joelle. I don't have to turn my head to feel Joelle's grin. "But do not despair. There are a number of juicy roles for both men and women in this production, and I will need all of you." Ms. Godwin whirls around and taps the pile of stapled packets stacked neatly on the edge of the stage. "This packet contains a summary of the play and a description of each role and key scenes. Auditions will take place next Tuesday, promptly at three thirty p.m. No excuses. No sob stories. No whining." She smiles tightly, gathers her fluttery, feathery, flowy clothes around her, and proceeds right up the aisle past us, shoes clicking clicking clicking till she reaches the very back of the house. After the door slams behind her, everyone crowds the stage, grabbing for a packet.

Joelle comes back with two: one for her and one for me. "Hamlet!" she says. "This is so cool!"

"Yeah," I say. "As long as she's doesn't want me to do some minimalist thing. Like the stage is set with one coffee table and a telephone or whatever."

"Who cares?" she says, flipping through the pages of the packet and scanning the lines. "You never minded before."

"I need something to build. Venetian canals. Castles. Throne rooms. The Vatican. I need to be distracted, Joelle."

"Bastards," Joelle murmurs, and squeezes my arm, but her heart's not in it. Her heart's with Hamlet, brooding somewhere in Denmark. She turns a page in Ms. Godwin's packet. "To be or not to be," she says, her voice soft. "That is the question."

I sigh. "One of them, anyway."

After Drama Club I start to walk home, but I'm stricken with the thought that my mom might be waiting to talk to me about sex and how beautiful it is with the right people. She's bound to have a speech ready by now. Maybe even some websites she wants me to visit, the name of a gynecologist she's made an appointment with, or a few "intriguing" books—*Sex in the City: Maintaining Your Selfhood in a Corrupt Culture; Things My Mother Never Told Me; Sugar and Spice: Teenage Girls Talk about Life, Love, and Sex.*

My mom. My dad. Books by PhD's. Doctors with gloved fingers and neutral expressions and why-don't-you-tell-me-about-it's.

I turn around and walk instead to the strip mall down the road from the school. There's not much there: a card store, an ice cream store, an electronics store, a beauty supply store, and one of those places that sells Christmas trees and ornaments in the winter and lawn furniture and Frisbees in the summer. We used to come here a lot in sixth grade to hang out at the Carvel ice cream store and make fun of the names on the cakes, which sounded vaguely porn-ish to us easily amused pre-teens. The Hug Me the Bear cake. The Fudgie the Whale cake. And our favorite, Cookie Puss, which was some unidentifiable mystery alien creature with an ice cream cone for a nose. *Cookie Puss! Cookie Puss!* we'd growl over and over again, until the ice cream guy chased us out of the store.

I'm not in the mood for ice cream. Instead, I decide to

wander up and down the aisles of the Christmas place, poking at the fake trees and the lighted candy canes. They have an entire section devoted to Nativity scenes of all sizes and shapes, and I go there to check them out. Jesus, Mary, and Joseph in plastic; Jesus, Mary, and Joseph in wire; Jesus, Mary, and Joseph in wood. I say "hey" to all the Jesuses. *Hey, baby.* It's what I used to say to my mom's stomach when she was pregnant with Henry. I don't remember it; I read about it in a notebook I found hidden at the back of my mother's closet. She was only pregnant for five months before she lost him. The last entry in the book, the entry my mother wrote a few months after Henry died, said that I kept patting her belly, saying *Hey, baby, Hey baby, Hey baby.* She wrote that the last time I said it, my father put his face in his hands and cried. She wrote that I never said it again.

I get tired of walking around, so I slump down on a bale of hay in one of the life-sized Nativity scenes. I glance around. Mary seems smug, Joseph seems stunned, and baby Jesus looks like a glowworm in a blanket, but the bale of hay is the perfect place for a girl to hide from her mother, her father, the world. I gather my hair up in a loose bun at the back of my head, yank one of the elastics I always wear around on my wrist and wind it around the knot. Then I dig in my backpack for *Much Ado About Nothing* and start reading.

"You can't sit here," a voice says.

I look up, confused. I must have been sitting for a while, because my butt's asleep. The guy standing over me is maybe fifteen, but I don't recognize him. He's wearing a uniform vest the red of his numerous zits. His name tag says "Walt."

"What's up, Walt?"

Walt is short and skinny, with a very prominent Adam's apple. He also has a serious hair-gel fetish. He's probably the one who set up the Nativity scene that I am ruining with my presence. I'm pretty sure I'm not holy enough to guest-star in any Nativity scenes.

"You can't just sit there," he warbles. "This isn't a library."

"I know that," I say. I wonder if his hair is stiff enough to pop a balloon. "I was just resting my legs."

"Yeah, well. You can't do that, either." He scratches at a pimple on his nose. "You've been back here for forty-five minutes."

"I have not," I say.

"Have too."

I don't feel like getting up. I don't feel like talking to Walt. I don't feel like talking to anyone. "There's no one in the store. What do you care if I sit here or not?"

"*I* don't care," Walt says. "My boss cares. He told me to tell you to leave. He thinks you're going to steal something."

"Like what?"

"How should I know?" he says.

"Think I'm going to smuggle out the baby Jesus over there?"

"Maybe."

"And why does he look like a glowworm, anyway?"

"Like a what?"

"Never mind," I say. I don't know why I'm torturing Zit Boy. It's not his fault that I'm in a pissy mood and that his boss thinks I'm going to make off with the Virgin Mary. I shove my book back into my bag and stand up, my butt tingling painfully. "I'm going."

"Good," he says.

I feel a weird little snap at the back of my neck, and suddenly my hair falls down. I shake my head and pluck the broken elastic off my shoulder. I'm about to fling it to the floor when I see Walt's face. He's smiling.

"What?" I say.

"Nothing," he says. But he's still smiling.

"What?" I say again, louder.

"You're that girl, aren't you?"

"I'm *a* girl, if that's what you mean," I say, though I know. Of course I know.

"That senior girl. I saw the picture," he says. The smile is now a smirk. There should be some sort of law against smirking. You should have to be at least eighteen to do it. It should require a license. "Everyone at school has seen that picture," he's saying.

"I don't know what you're talking about," I say. But he's watching me tug at my hair, and he doesn't believe me.

"Sure," he says.

This kid doesn't even shave yet. He probably has a penis the size of a pencil eraser. "What are you talking about?" I say, practically shouting.

"Nothing," he says. He's starting to enjoy himself. He's bouncing up on his toes to make himself taller.

"That's right, *nothing*," I say, practically spitting. "You know nothing."

Bounce, bounce, bounce. God should strike him dead. Or at least explode all his zits at once. "You need to look into something for those pimples," I tell him, turning to leave. "I saw a commercial on TV for some stuff that might help."

"Maybe *you* should be on TV. Or in one of those movies. You'd get paid, anyway," he calls after me. I walk faster, but not fast enough. Just as I make it to the front counter, where some gray-haired man is frowning sternly, I hear Zit Boy call: "Or maybe you like to do it for free?"

Okay. Fine. Christmas store, bad idea. Nativity scene, bad idea. I push open the glass door with my foot and storm outside. I know I should just go home, but I think that maybe Cookie Puss and Fudgie the Whale could use some company. But what's the first thing I see?

A green minivan parked right next to the ice cream store. A minivan that looks a lot like Luke's mom's minivan, a van that Luke sometimes used when he had lots of stuff to cart around, or when he wanted a little portable privacy. I'm assaulted by flashbacks. Hands slipping up the back of my shirt, looking for the bra clasp. Fingers scrabbling at the front of my jeans. The smell of carpeting and warm skin. And then newer memories: slamming the door on Luke at the party, my picture on the cell phone, his stone face as he passed me in the hallway.

I'm standing frozen on the walk when I see the door of the ice cream shop swing open. I don't have time to think, to consider if it really is Luke's mom's green van and if that really is Luke coming out of the ice cream store with another one of the half-vanilla, half-chocolate milkshakes he lives on. I do the only thing I can: I duck into Sally Beauty Supply. The choppy-haired punk girl at the counter looks up from her magazine, looks me up and down, and then looks down at the magazine again. Well, here's someone who obviously hasn't seen the infamous photograph. Hallelujah. Sighing in relief, I begin fake-browsing the shelves. I have my choice of cheap lipsticks in every shade known to woman and hair clips with beads, sparkles, or feathers, as well as curlers, crimpers, dryers, tweezers, and other instruments of torture. I pick through nail files and polishes, shampoos and conditioners, gels and mousses. I make faces at the wig heads and then wonder if there are hidden cameras documenting everything I'm not buying. Moving on to the dyes, I marvel at the colors. Vampire Red. Purple Passion. Too Blue. Flamingo. Fade to Black. For some reason, I like the last color the best, like how it looks, all inky and thick in the bottles. I grab a couple, one in each hand, just to look as if I'm actually shopping, doing something other than hiding from other people's mom's vans.

"You're going to need developer with that."

I whip around and see the girl from the counter standing there. With her plaid pants and a "Luv A Nerd" T-shirt, she's paired black socks with green rubber flip-flops. I'm momentarily stunned by her fashion choices, and by the Oreo-sized plugs piercing her ears. "What?"

"Developer," she says. She pulls a big bottle of white stuff from the shelf. "You can't use the dye unless you mix it with this."

"Oh," I say. "But . . ."

"Have you ever dyed your hair before?" she asks me. Her hair is Flamingo, with Purple Passion bangs. She's clearly an expert.

"Uh, no, but . . ."

She plucks a bottle of dye from my hand. "I know it says 'Fade to Black,' but it's really a very dark brown. I don't know why they don't call it something else. I always thought that Dirt would be a good name."

"Dirt?" I say. I would never want my hair to be something called Dirt.

"You should probably get some gloves." She thrusts a box of rubber gloves at me. "The whole box is only five bucks, so it's worth it. Especially if you dye your hair again. And you will, believe me. It's addictive." She hands me a little plastic bowl and something that looks a lot like a paintbrush. "Use this to mix the dye in. Equal parts dye and developer. Use the brush to paint the dye on. Start at the roots and work down to the ends. Wait twenty-five minutes and wash it all out until the water comes clear." She eyes me critically, and I see that she's even dyed her eyebrows Flamingo to match her hair. "You have a ton of hair. And it's so blond. Is that natural?"

"Yeah," I say. "But I'm not sure . . ."

She pulls another bottle of Fade to Black from the shelf. "You're going to need more." She looks at the pile I have in my arms and laughs. "I guess I should help you carry the stuff up to the front."

"Thanks," I say. "But I really haven't decided whether . . ."

She turns abruptly and walks to the front of the store. I follow, because I don't know what else to do. She moves behind the register and faces me. "I say go for it," she tells me. "If you don't like it, you can just chop it all off, right?"

I dump the stuff on the counter, wondering how I'm going to get out of the store without buying a thousand dollars' worth of products. "It took me years to grow my hair. I can't just chop it off."

Flamingo is amused. "Why not? Is it sacred or something? Are you Samson? Besides, think about how different you'll look with dark hair. I swear no one will recognize you."

I'm sure that everyone would recognize me if my hair were blue, with lime-green polka dots. But then, the thought that it might take people a few extra seconds makes me hesitate. Flamingo moves in for the kill. "I dye my hair all the time, and it works out fine for me. If I don't like what's going on, if things are crappy or just boring, I make my hair another color and I'm a new person. Easiest thing in the world." She smiles at me, a different kind of smile than the ones I've been getting the last few days. A sweet smile, a friendly smile, an I-don't-know-who-you-are-and-I-couldn't-care-less smile. She starts to ring up the stuff, and I don't stop her. "Don't worry," she says. "You're going to be great."

We Interrupt
This Program for
a Special Report

I'm twenty-five bucks poorer when I walk
home, and I'm not happy about it. I don't know
why I let some punk girl in flip-flops talk me into
buying stuff that will turn my hair the color of dirt.
Dirt! And who is so dumb that they believe dyeing
your hair can make you a whole new person? I
fumble around in the bag for the receipt.

Great. She forgot to put one in there, and I forgot to ask for it. Twenty-five bucks down the tube because I couldn't face Luke's mom's van.

My dad's not happy, either. Apparently, he went to a lawyer and got some answers on the legal front. Since no one's face is visible in the picture, he tells us at dinner, it would be difficult to prosecute anyone for sending it.

"He did say that we could at least threaten to sue," my dad says. "Since it's probably a kid who sent the picture around, we could shake him up."

"What will that do?" I say.

"What do you mean, what will it do?" my dad says, chewing his broccoli vigorously. "It will stop the little monster from doing it again."

"Dad, I don't even know who sent it."

"Did you ask that boy?"

I want to say *What boy?* but I know what boy. "No," I say. "I don't want to talk to him."

"I wouldn't want to talk to him, either, after what he did to you," my dad says. "Now that I'm thinking about it, you shouldn't talk to him. You should let me talk to him. *I'll* shake him up." For a second, he looks so mad that I worry he'll find Luke and rip his arms off. And maybe some other key parts, too. Not that it wouldn't be a *teeny* bit satisfying, but I know that if my dad even talks to Luke or his parents I will never, ever hear the end of this. Everyone will just blame me anyway.

"Dad, I don't want you to do anything," I say. "I want to forget about it."

"Forget about it?" he says. He turns to my mother. "Elaine, will you talk some sense into her, please?" He scoops up his plate and practically throws it into the sink. "I have to look at some prom gown catalogs." He stalks from the room.

I push my broccoli around my plate. "Dad's freaking out."

"We're all freaking out," my mom says. "You're not eating."

"I don't like broccoli."

"You love broccoli."

"I love the cheese sauce that goes on the broccoli. I never liked the broccoli."

"I'm worried about you." My mom starts clearing the table. "I called my doctor. He had an appointment available, and I—"

I knew it! I start moaning: "*Mom . . .*"

"Audrey," she says, her voice firm. "If you're sexually active, you need to see a doctor. This is not debatable."

I wince at the phrase "sexually active." So weird and vague. So not sexy. So not the way I'd describe anything I've ever done. "Do I have to go to a man?"

"He's a good doctor," she says. "I've been going to him for years. But if you want me to make some more calls—"

"Fine," I say, too embarrassed for the both of us to argue. "When's the appointment?"

"Next Friday. Four o'clock."

"You're taking me, right?" I say, suddenly terrified that my *dad* will want to do it.

"Yes," she says. "You might not be comfortable talking to us about these things, but I want you to be honest with the doctor."

I nod.

"I mean it," she says.

"I know." I feel like I'm at the doctor's already, splayed out under the bright lights. I can hear the questions now: *Are you sexually active, Ms. Porter? When did you first become sexually active? How often are you sexually active? Did you know that sexual activities occurring in green vans are more likely to result in hair the color of dirt?*

"Can I ask you a question?" my mom says. She doesn't wait for me to say yes before she says, "Did you care about that boy?"

I feel a flare of anger at this, and then it's gone. "No. I just picked him up off the street."

"Audrey . . ." she says.

"Yes, I liked him. Of course I liked him. Jeez. What do you think?"

"I'm sorry," she says. "You read magazines and see TV shows about what kids are doing. Scary things. Bets and games and contests. Girls doing things just to be popular. All that stuff on the Internet."

I don't say anything; I can only imagine what was on the latest episode of *Oprah*.

Mom blows a curl from her cheek. "This is exactly what makes parents crazy," she says.

"What is?"

"This. All of this. One day you're building little cities out of toothpicks, and the next . . ." She trails off. I finish her thought in my head. *And the next you're blowing random guys. What a world! It must be the rap music! The video games! Someone alert the media! We need to do a Special Report!*

But that's not what she says. "The next minute, you find out that your child isn't a child anymore, that she's being confronted with things that could hurt her or even change her life forever. I speak from experience." Again she tries to tell me that sex is beautiful, but that's not what her face says. Her face says that sex is kind of icky and sort of frightening. Something that you have to gear up for. Something that requires medical attention. Maybe it's only beautiful for people over a certain age. Or maybe it's beautiful for everyone other than somebody's daughter.

But she's still forging ahead. "You open yourself up to so much," she says. "I'm not just talking about pregnancy and disease, I'm talking about your heart. I'm talking about people breaking it. It's wonderful and natural," she says. "But only with people you can trust."

She can't tell me how you know who you can trust. "What, do they have neon signs on their foreheads or something?"

She looks depressed and defeated, and I feel bad. She's trying to help and I won't let her. Why can't I let her? "This is why the pastors at church say it's smart to wait," she says.

As far as I can tell, the pastors at the church like to talk about everything *but* sex, except to tell us to "save ourselves for our husbands and wives." Both pastors are at least sixty years old. Who says they can even remember sex? And besides, me and my mom both know how *I* came to be. An unplanned little bomb that blew up in my parents' senior year of college. I try not to sound pissed when I say, "Is that what you think?"

She's been wandering around the kitchen, shifting things—the fork here, the tub of butter there—but not really putting anything away. She gives up and sits back down at the table. "I think it's best to wait as long as you can. Until you find someone you love."

"So you waited for Dad," I say.

My mother looks extremely uncomfortable, as if she's suddenly been stricken with intestinal cramps. "This is not about me. I'm just one person."

Whoa. "You didn't wait?"

"What I did or didn't do is not the point," she tells me. "Every person is unique." She looks down at the table and brushes some crumbs into her palm.

Now that we're talking, I realize that I don't want all the sordid details, that I really don't want to know who my mom was with and when. I mean, yuck. Then I realize that it's probably how she's thinking of me—my daughter, sex, yuck. For something that's supposed to be all God-given and Song of Solomon and comfort-me-with-apples fabulous, it feels about as beautiful as drinking from a toilet bowl. At least that's what it feels like afterward, when someone's taken a picture of you and decorated the world with it and your mom is about to drag you off to the clinic for tests.

I notice that she's not asked me exactly the kinds of "sexual activities" I've participated in, whether or not I'm still a virgin. She doesn't want to know, either. I guess if I could do this one thing, I could do almost anything.

She's right.

"You think I'm a slut."

Her head whips up. "No, I do not think you're a slut. I absolutely do not think that. And neither does your father. How could we? We love you. And nothing has changed that. Nothing will ever ever change that."

"I feel like a slut," I say. "I didn't before. But I do now."

"Oh, honey," she says, and grabs my hands. She squeezes so hard that my knuckles go white.

Talking about sex totally wrings my mother out; she goes to bed at about eight thirty. I'm so tense and befreaked that I have a hard time getting into my homework, but when I do, it's like I disappear for a while, let all the facts and figures scour my brain, scrub it clean and light. Cat Stevens curls up in my lap as I read, purring so hard that I feel the vibrations in my fingertips.

Hours have gone by before I look at the clock again. After midnight, I put the books away and sit at my computer. I tool around my friends' blogs for a while, occasionally pushing Cat Stevens out of the way when he decides to do his happy-kitty parade march in front of the screen. Joelle has publicly threatened to murder the person who took the photograph of me and Luke and offered a "lunch date at the restaurant of your choice" to anyone who has any information on the "perpetrator," and then goes on to babble about starring in *Hamlet*, even though it hasn't been cast yet. On her blog, Ash dissects horribly depressing lyrics, which means that she has her favorite angryshriekypunky songs on a loop again. She's probably sitting in her bedroom, enveloped by a cloud of gray smoke that she's only halfheartedly trying to blow out the open window, cutting up whatever photos of Jimmy she hasn't already cut up. Or maybe she's just cutting up the pieces into smaller pieces.

I don't have as many messages as before, and for some reason I'm able to read them. They're the same crap, but it's like they're talking about some other girl. Pam Markovitz or Cindy Terlizzi or someone. They don't even make me mad. I think of Ash, how she kept asking, *Aren't you mad? Don't you want to know who did this?* and wonder why I'm not mad, why I can't seem to get there for longer than two seconds, why I haven't been spending my time making lists of possible suspects, why the first thought I had after I found out about the picture was my history test. I should be mad. I should be something.

Someone has sent me another copy of my picture, and I can't help but stare at it. On my big computer screen, it's incredibly clear. I'm amazed that it's me. I'd never gone down on anyone before, never really wanted to before. The only reason I had any clue how to do it is because me and Ash had once Googled for instructions, which Ash then demonstrated on an ice pop. Back when she did goofy stuff like that, back when she and Jimmy were in love.

I touch my mouth, the way you touch your mouth after you've been kissed, the way I did when Luke first kissed me at Ash's party at the end of the summer. I can still taste the salt on my tongue, but I can't connect the picture to me—all that striped blond hair shining; all of that pale, naked skin glowing in the dark. I look at Luke's hands, how they clutch the bedspread, like if he doesn't hang on tight, like if he doesn't sit as still as he can, something crazy-awful could happen. He could float up to the ceiling. He could fly out the window. He could separate into trillions of atoms and disperse into the air.

My eyes wander from the picture to the corner of my room where I've dumped the bag from Sally Beauty Supply, then back to the picture again. Bag, picture. Bag, picture.

Yeah, I should be mad. Or sad. Something. Anything. I jump up from my chair, grab the bag, and head to the bathroom.

Bad

At my high school, the DeSalvio boys are legend. First there was Jeff, four years ahead of Luke. Tallest of the three, Jeff had wheat-blond hair, midnight-blue eyes, and a butt you could bounce quarters off of. Girls—and, rumor has it, more than one teacher—practically threw themselves at him when he walked down the hall. But

Jeff was the nice one, the committed one. He dated a pretty but not gorgeous girl named Anna Pritchard for the last three years of high school, and on into college. We all figure they'll be married and procreating a month after they get their degrees, propagating the luscious DeSalvio genes to torment future generations of women.

After Jeff came Eric, otherwise known as Eric the Red because of his looks-like-it-came-from-a-box-but-didn't red hair and his wild Viking habits. Eric went through girls like Kleenex but was so smooth about it that no one seemed to mind too much (or they were so busy fighting each other that they forgot to get mad at him). Eric was thrown off the football team after he was caught on the field after dark with one of the cheerleaders. He claimed he was helping her practice some dance moves, but since none of the cheerleading routines required that the cheerleaders go bottomless, no one was buying it.

And then there was Luke. Even though we'd spent years speculating, no one really seemed to know him. He was just as popular as his brothers, but you couldn't pin him down—he wasn't exactly straight-edge like Jeff and he wasn't exactly wild like Eric. Rumors flew about who he'd been with at which party, but he rarely hooked up with anyone for long and he never offered up any details himself. People whispered: *He's way hot, but he's a huge player, he spent two hours locked in a walk-in closet with Barbara Morganstein and then the next day asked Georgia Herman to the spring dance, he's really nice once you get to know him, but he doesn't care about anyone but himself, avoid him like the plague but do anything to get his attention.* Come here, go away, come back, wait!

After Ash's end-of-the-summer-party and my first marathon make-out session with Luke, I understood the confusion. I *was* the confusion. I walked around as if I'd been hit in the head with a falling piano. My speech was garbled as a drunk's, I tripped over my own feet, I ran over our garbage cans during a driving lesson. My mother became terrified that I had a vision problem or perhaps some kind of spectacular, inoperable brain tumor after she watched me walk smack into a closed door. For the third time. (I ended up at a specialist's.)

I couldn't think of anything else but Luke. The way he smelled. The way he kissed. The way his hands felt combing through my hair. My skin alternately tingled and flamed, and my bottom lip swelled up to twice the size because I couldn't stop nibbling on it.

I was insane.

Ash was like, "*Verdammt.* You're acting like you've never been with a guy!" I had, but not in the same way. Not even close. Before Luke, it was all so technical. Did you kiss? Did you French? For how long? Did he try anything else? Did you let him? Would you let him go further? Even when I was in the middle of kissing some-one, even when I liked that person or thought I did, my brain was always chattering, chattering, chattering: *I hope my breath's okay God why is he flicking his tongue so fast it's making me dizzy what time is it I hope it's not after eleven because my dad will kill me if I don't get home by eleven is he trying to get up my shirt already why didn't I wear my nice bra why did I have to wear the stretched-out old cotton one it makes me look all droopy like an old lady maybe Mom will take me to get some new bras and underwear too maybe this weekend but I can't go this weekend because I have to write my "Scarlet Letter" paper and I have a math test on Tuesday and I don't think I even want him up my shirt it tickles he's an idiot he can't work the clasp and I want to laugh and what if he tries to get in my pants I have my period oh God YUCK!!*

Kissing Luke, I'd felt the opposite, my brain going all hushed and quiet, murmuring things like *oh* and *wow* and *hmmmm*. Ash got worried. She told me about his rep, she told me not to get too crazy, she told me that just because there was one hookup didn't mean there would be another one.

The second time came just a week after the first. Pool party at Christina Webster's. Christina worked with Ash on the school literary magazine, where they selected the best nobody-understands-me-I-am-lost-in-the-darknessso-must-wear-chains-and-way-too-much-eye-makeup poems from the dozens upon dozens that were submitted every year. Christina was not particularly lost, not particularly dark, and didn't wear nearly enough black eyeshadow for Ash's tastes, but she did have a large in-ground pool in her backyard and parents who weren't all that interested in her, so Christina found herself with a lot of new friends every summer.

Anyway, me and Ash and Joelle showed up around three o'clock. Joelle immediately peeled down to her dental-floss bikini and demanded that we help her put on her sunscreen. (No real tans for Joelle; she claimed that they ruined the skin.) Two girls lotioning up an almost-naked, soon-to-be movie star is enough of a show for any high school guy; we were instantly surrounded by about eighteen dripping-wet boys in long board shorts, demanding to know if we wanted anything—coffee? tea? or me? Ha!! Joelle batted her eyelashes and Ash rolled her eyes while I scanned the party for Luke. I was desperate to see him again, thought I might just hyperventilate and die if I didn't. And then there he was, climbing out of the deep end, and I thought I might hyperventilate and die anyway. His shorts were a neon shade of orange that somehow perfectly set off the golden tan (I guess he didn't think that tans ruined the skin) and the sun-bleached hair. The body, that not-too-big, not-too-small body, was fatless and sculpted, the most delicious-looking abs in the known universe rippling from his nearly hairless chest down into the waistband of his bathing suit. Luke reached up and slicked his wet hair from his face. I nearly toppled out of my chair when I saw that the delicate undersides of his arms were a shade paler than the rest of him.

I felt a sharp elbow in the ribs. "Stop staring," Ash hissed. "You look like some kind of maniac stalker."

"She *is* a maniac stalker," Joelle said. "You missed a spot on my shoulder blade. I can feel it."

"Then you can just do it yourself," Ash said, throwing the bottle of sunscreen on the ground next to the deck chair. "This scene is straight out of a porn flick."

"Did somebody say 'porn flick'?" one of the eighteen guys said.

"Yeah," said Ash. "It's playing at the shallow end. Why don't you dive for it?"

"And what do you know about porn flicks, young lady?" said Joelle. She lifted her hand and waved at Luke, who waved back.

"Don't wave," I said, under my breath.

"Why not?" Joelle whispered. "Don't you want him to come here?"

"Don't talk so loud," I said.

Joelle wasn't listening; she was waggling her fingers at Luke, motioning him over. "Audrey, hurry up and take off your shirt so he can see your bikini."

"Joelle!"

Another of the eighteen: "Yeah, take off your shirt, Audrey."

"My God," said Ash, who was wearing a beater and cutoff jeans that she would swim in.

"What?" said Joelle. "He shouldn't see her bikini? What's wrong with her bikini? I helped her pick it out."

"I'm not sure I want anyone to see my bikini," I said.

The eighteen: "We want to see it!"

"Will you losers get the hell away from us?" Ash snapped. When Ash snapped, people usually obeyed. There were a few grumbles, but the eighteen drifted away.

I didn't have time to take off my shirt even if I'd wanted to; by the time the eighteen cleared off, Luke was standing at the end of my lounge chair.

Joelle put a palm over her eyes and squinted up at him. "Hi, Luke, what's up?" she said brightly, as if they'd been dear friends since birth.

"Hey, Joelle, not much," he said. He nodded at Ash. "Any new piercings?"

Ash smiled. "Not today."

"I think Nardo's around here somewhere, in case you're interested."

Ash shrugged; Nardo had been calling and texting her since Joelle's party, but she was ignoring him. She said that it was because he was too straight-edge, she said she preferred her boys in a bit of guyliner, she said she didn't need a boyfriend, but I thought it was because she was afraid to be hurt. She got pissed when I'd said so, so I wasn't planning on going there again.

Luke smiled at me, but didn't say anything. He sat down on the end of my chair so that I had to bend my knees a little to make room. "So, Joelle," he said, "how's business? Any new TV shows?"

Joelle wrinkled her pert little nose. "No. Not that I haven't been auditioning every thirteen seconds. My agent has a lead on a commercial spot, some perfume or whatever, so maybe something will happen with that. I'd rather not do commercials, you know, but work is work. Everything counts."

"I guess you have to sacrifice for your art," said Luke.

Joelle clutched at her chest. "That's so true!"

Without looking at me, Luke reached out and put his hand around my ankle. His thumb gently rubbed the knob of bone that stuck out. My breath caught in my throat.

Joelle's eyes flicked to my ankle, and a perfectly evil grin spread across her face. She reached down and picked up the bottle of sunscreen that Ash had thrown to the ground. "I keep telling Audrey that she has to be more careful with her skin," she said. "Why don't you put some of this on her?" She handed Luke the bottle.

Luke looked at me. "Do you want some?"

It seemed like a loaded question.

"Okay," I said.

"Start with her back," said Joelle. "Audrey, take off your shirt so that he can do your shoulders."

"Jesus, Joelle," Ash said, "why do you keep asking Audrey to take off her clothes?"

"What?" said Joelle, her eyes wide and innocent.

To Luke, I said: "Joelle secretly wants to be a director."

"Yeah," said Ash, snorting. "Of adult films."

"I hear there's money in that," Luke said. He held up the bottle of sunscreen and waited for me to take my shirt off. I guessed there was nothing else for me to do except take it off, so I did. Luke touched the strap of my turquoise halter top right where it hit my collarbone. "I like this."

If I looked into his eyes I thought I might spontaneously combust. "Thanks," I said to the space between his eyebrows.

"I helped her pick it out," said Joelle.

"You have good taste," Luke said.

I swung around to a sitting position and lifted my hair. I noticed that a few of the girls around the pool were watching this operation intently and tried to keep my expression neutral, like, Oh, ho hum, another hot guy lathering me up with sunscreen, yawn. But then Luke's warm hands were on my shoulders and on my neck and skating down my spine, and I was positive that I looked like I had somehow ingested a ball of fire that was slowly expanding in my gut and roaring outward to every limb. Despite the August heat and the weird burning in my stomach, my skin exploded into goose bumps.

Joelle chattered on about a disastrous grape-juice commercial she did when she was six as Luke smoothed lotion over my back, shoulders, and arms. "We had no idea that I was allergic to grapes," Joelle said, "until I got sick all over the director."

"That's pretty funny," Luke said to her. "Did they fire you?"

At the word "fire," I shuddered a little. Luke pressed his thumbs into the muscles along my neck until I relaxed.

"Amazingly enough," said Joelle, "they didn't. I did three commercials for them. Go figure. *I* would have fired me. I mean, puking on the director's shoes? Not the way to get ahead."

Luke's hands slid around my waist and gave my stomach two quick (too-quick) swipes. "They must have liked you a lot," he said to her. To me he said, "Sit back." I dropped my hair and leaned back in the chair so that he could do my legs. He started at my feet and moved upward, bending my leg so that he could get the underside as well as the front. I could barely keep myself from howling out loud. As his palms circled upward toward the hem of the white denim skirt I wore over my bikini bottoms, I wondered where he would stop, or if he would just keep going until he was publicly molesting me and I would be faced with the choice of kicking him or letting him. His fingers slid briefly yet chastely under my skirt to get the tops of my thighs, and then he was done. The finishing touch was the brush of his thumb down the bridge of my nose and across each cheekbone.

He snapped the top of the bottle closed and held it out to me. "There you go," he said.

I took the bottle. "Thanks," I squeaked.

"So do you guys want to swim?" he asked.

"Maybe later," said Joelle. "But you go ahead." We watched as he ran for the diving board, gracefully loping back to the rest of his kind—the young, the proud, the penised.

After Luke was safely back in the pool, I exhaled heavily. "You are an evil, evil, evil chick, Joelle. Evil. E. Vil."

"That's what they tell me."

"I've just been mauled."

Joelle shrieked with laughter loud enough to make the other girls around the pool glare at us. "And you enjoyed every minute."

Ash merely shook her head. "Girl, you have it bad."

"Do you blame her?" Joelle demanded.

"I don't have it so bad," I said. I was literally burning up. I stood, unbuttoned my skirt, and dropped it around my feet, happy that the bikini bottoms were boy-cut shorts and not one of Joelle's dental-floss numbers.

"Look what you've done, Joelle. You've turned our sweet little honors student into a stripper. Audrey, you should see your face right now."

I sat down again. "What do you mean?"

"You look like a puddle of melted wax," Ash said. "Oh, never mind. Don't say I didn't warn you."

"Leave her alone," Joelle said. "When was the last time she had a bit of a rubdown?"

"Why didn't you get your own rubdown, if that's what you're into, Ms. Movie Star?" Ash said.

Joelle adjusted one of the miniscule triangles covering her sizable boobs. "We're not talking about me. And why aren't you off looking for that guy you hooked up with last week? What's-his-name? Nardo?"

"Who?" said Ash.

I lay back down and closed my eyes. I stopped listening to them and tried to listen to myself. I told myself that Ash was right, one hookup didn't necessarily mean another one. It was stupid to get messed up with someone like him, someone who could have anyone he wanted (and probably did). I heard the happy squeals of this girl and that girl as the guys tossed them around the pool—"Luke! Stop it! *Lu-uuke!*" *See?* I said to myself.

You had your fun, now move on, leave it alone. But just a half hour later, when I felt a brief squeeze on my big toe and heard Luke's low voice saying "See you," I felt like I might drown in disappointment. I sat up to see Luke walking through the gate at the side of the house. As if my chair had suddenly grown thorns, as if my feet had developed brains and wills of their own, I jumped out of the chair and followed.

"Audrey," Ash said, but I ignored her and ran after him in my bare feet. I caught up with him at his car, an enormous green van.

"Hey," I said.

He turned around and smiled. "Hey."

"Are you leaving?"

"Yeah," he said. "I have to work tonight."

Work? *He works,* I thought. *Some place where other people tell him what to do.* It was oddly fascinating. "Where do you work?"

"Rock Garden Restaurant. Here's a tip for you: never eat there. The cooks don't."

"Don't what?"

"Cook." He looked at his watch. "I'd love to hang out longer, but my shift starts at five. I have to go home and change first."

"Oh," I said stupidly. I stood there, suddenly aware that while he'd put on a dry T-shirt, I was standing in the street wearing very few, very small items of clothing. I wrapped my arms around myself—to hide myself, to hug myself, I wasn't sure. My nipples felt like bullets against my forearms.

"I really like that bathing suit," he said.

"You already said that," I told him.

He blinked slowly, as if his lashes were made of lead. "It's worth repeating."

"Oh," I said again. The ball of fire was back, threatening to take over my body, the block, the planet. I'd never been so attracted to a guy in my life. It was like there were tiny magnets in my mitochondria, tugging me toward him. Without thinking, I took two giant steps forward.

"Well, hi," he said when I was standing under his nose.

I lifted my face and breathed him in. "Hi and goodbye," I said. "Do I get a kiss?"

Yes, I do.

The Other Audrey

After an hour and a half of labor plus three bottles of dye, one oversized bottle of developer, one paintbrush thingy, and a hand mirror so that I can see the back of my head, I'm no longer a blonde. It takes another forty-five minutes to scrub the bathroom sink and tub free of splotches and smears of dye I'd gotten absolutely everywhere. Only then do I allow myself to take a serious look.

My hair is less the color of dirt and more the black-brown of coffee grounds. Next to all that dark hair, my skin looks paler yet somehow brighter, my eyes gold and lionlike. It's me. And isn't me at all. For some reason, it's different than dyeing your hair a fake color, green or blue or hot pink, the kind of color that people use to piss off their parents or scare old ladies or prove to all the other teenagers that you are so much more wild and crazy and unique than they are. This is a normal color that could be found in nature. So it *could* be real. I could be this fierce coffee-haired person walking around, this other Audrey, a mirror image of myself. Someone who's never fallen in lust with Luke DeSalvio and so was never "sexually active" with him and never had her photograph zipping around cyberspace. Someone who's never been humiliated in front of her entire school and her own parents. I go to bed at three a.m., Stevie the Purr Monster draped across my chest. For the first time in days, I fall asleep as soon as my head hits the pillow.

Four hours later, I drag myself downstairs, Stevie at my heels. My parents are both sitting at the breakfast table, talking in low voices. They both stop and stare when I come into the room. My parents both have brown hair. They always thought my blond hair was this special thing, like a present they got when I was born.

They aren't happy.

"Audrey!" says my mom.

"Your hair!" says my dad.

I grab the nearest box of cereal and flop into my seat. Stevie jumps on the table and my dad shoos him off. "It will grow out, okay? Don't give me a hard time about it."

They look at each other, then back at me. "But," my dad says, "your hair was so beautiful."

"It still is," I say.

He doesn't know how to respond to that.

A few minutes later, my mom says, "It does set off your eyes."

"Thanks, Mom."

"If you do it again, maybe you could think about putting in some red highlights."

"Red what? What are you talking about?" says my dad. "Why . . ." He starts again. "*What* made you change your hair?"

"No reason. This crazy store clerk talked me into it. When I get sick of it, I can always dye it back. Or shave it off."

"Shave it off?" My dad is really becoming alarmed now.

"She's not going to shave it off, John," my mom says.

"How do you know?" I say.

My mom sighs and rolls her eyes toward the ceiling.

I haven't seen that in a while, and it makes me feel better. Then she ruins the mood by saying, "Remember, you have your doctor's appointment at the end of next week."

In the car, Ash can't get over me. "Holy *Scheisse!*" she says. "What the hell did you do to yourself?"

"I figure that if I have to be all dark and brooding, I should look the part."

"You even did your eyebrows! I've never done my eyebrows."

"Yeah. The package said that you weren't supposed to, that you could, I don't know, go blind or something if you got the stuff in your eyes, but I thought I'd look really dumb with blond eyebrows and brown hair."

Ash leans back in her seat and considers me. "You know what? I like it. It's pretty cool. Hot, actually."

"Thanks."

As she turns into the school parking lot, she says, "But it's not like people won't recognize you. I mean, they still might be talking about that stupid picture. So . . ."

"I know," I tell her. "I get it. It's not a disguise. I just wanted a change, that's all."

But it does work as a disguise, at least a little bit. Some people float by me without seeming to see me, and a lot of others do double takes. I still get comments about the picture, I still hear whispers behind my back, but I keep telling myself that in a few weeks they'll forget. Someday soon, someone will write something outrageous and personal and maybe disgusting about someone else on a blog or a text message or chat, people will get pissed and the rumors will spread, and I'll be old news, no matter what color my hair is. I'll rack up the A's, I'll work on the set for *Hamlet*—even if there's only a coffee table and a telephone, it will be the best coffee table and telephone that the audience has ever seen. By April, I'll know where I'm going to college; then I can pack up and be off. See ya, kids. Bye-bye, high school. I'll leave this photograph behind while the gargoyle who took it will slink off to whatever circle of hell waits for him.

So I read, I study, I study some more. I admire my toothpick village and wish I were young enough to want to add to it, to disappear into a tiny little house or a train or a windmill. I slog from class to class to class. I'm more chilly than Chilly, I freeze him out. Except for Ash and Joelle, I freeze everyone out. By Friday afternoon, I've aced two tests and gotten an A plus on my *Much Ado About Nothing* paper from Mr. Lambright. Not bad. It seems that being a dirt-haired ho is pretty good for my grades. I seem to have mastered transitions.

On Saturday, I work in my parents' store, Angel, ringing up evening gowns and bridesmaids' dresses and wedding gowns. Normally, I do everything I can to help people find dresses that flatter them. This time, I tell everyone that they look beautiful even when it's not true, because this is what everyone wants to hear, because it's easier. I let three girls walk out of the store with feather boas. Yes, boas. Nobody wears boas—we've had the same four in stock since the Big Bang—but they didn't know that and I didn't tell them. I feel like a person with a rotten tooth or broken toe: it doesn't hurt enough to ignore the world, and it hurts too much to be patient with it.

Sunday morning. Church. Pastor Narcolepsy is even more hypnotic than usual, or maybe they put drugs in the communion wafers. The sermon is about how one can't really be a true Christian if one doesn't come to church. Which is fine and everything, except we are *at* church. Wouldn't it be better for the pastor to go find some people who aren't and give *them* the guilt trip? Like, say, go preach at the mall? I make the mistake of saying this to my parents on the way home.

"I don't know what's gotten into you," my dad says.

"What do you mean?" I say.

"Church is important."

"I didn't say it wasn't important. I'm just saying that it's weird to tell us to come to church when we're already there."

"The pastor was simply reminding us that regular worship is something that God wants," says my dad.

On the tip of my tongue: *Okay, who are you, and what have you done with my dad?* And: *How does anyone know what she wants?* But Dad finds my idea that God could be a woman amusing, and I really don't feel like amusing him. "Okay," I say, wondering why, all of a sudden, my dad is getting all churchy on me, babbling about what God wants—something he normally doesn't do except when we talk about the obvious stuff, like, Thou shalt not murder each other or steal one another's boyfriends/girlfriends or be nasty, greedy jerks who inflict your nasty, greedy jerkiness on other people. He's even grumbled at Mom's insistence that we go to church every week—he could open the store a few hours earlier if we didn't—and doesn't think it's funny when she tells him that she needs to repent for all those nice people she's killed with sewing scissors in her books.

I want to say, *Look, Dad, some of us aren't doing so well handling the big stuff that God wants, so going to church every three seconds seems pretty minor.* As a matter of fact, I think that church is one of those things that seems like a good idea but actually isn't that great in practice. Like, who would think that getting everyone together to talk and sing about God and goodness and love and Heaven and Jesus wouldn't be a fun thing? So why isn't it a fun thing, or even an interesting thing most of the time? Why isn't it more useful? Why don't they give practical lessons on how to deal with hot guys without having to wear a freaking chastity belt? Why are you always thinking about something else when you're there? Like the way the hook on your bra is digging into your back or the fact that the lady in front of you is wearing enough perfume to wipe out vast colonies of insects.

I don't know, I'll have to ask Joelle about temple. Maybe going to temple is different.

My dad looks in the rearview mirror, frowning deeply. He's been frowning deeply a lot. I have a name for that frown: it's the I-don't-know-you-anymore frown. The you-have-turned-into-someone-I-don't-understand frown.

Maybe I have.

Monday, study period. Chilly drops into the chair next to me, whistling. "Hey, baby. Don't think I got your name."

"Get away from me."

"Never heard that name before."

"You hear it all the time," I say.

"Do any photo shoots lately?"

I press my lips together and wait for the bell to ring so that he will Shut. Up. Already. Tayari Smith, gorgeous Tayari Smith, gives me a sympathetic look across the table, and in my reptilian brain I remember a story from eighth grade, something about how Tayari did something to or with some boy in the back of the bus on the way home from school and got suspended for it. I suddenly, desperately, want to be her friend. Maybe she can teach me what to do with my new dark hair. Maybe she can show me how to twist it and braid it and curl it into crazy corkscrews, a new do every day. Maybe I'll learn how to give other girls sympathetic looks over tables in study periods, I'll see how to get my dignity back.

"I was thinking," says Chilly. "You should send that picture in with your college applications. Might be the deciding factor. I know! You could take more photos. I can help."

Something about the way he says this makes me think. Did Chilly have a camera at that party? I don't remember a camera, but what if he did have one? What if he stole a camera and followed me upstairs? What if he snuck up behind us in the bedroom and . . .

"Was it you?" I say. My voice sounds like someone else's, like an echo from a radio.

"Me? What are you talking about? You can't even remember who you blew?"

"Did you take the picture?"

Chilly smiles. "What do you think?" He lifts his hands and makes like he's pressing a button.

I wasn't mad before, I wasn't, but that was the old Audrey, not the new, fierce coffee-haired Audrey. I hate Chilly, I *hate* him, and maybe he hates me, too, maybe he hates me more, but this is someone I went out with, someone I *made* out with. He was the first guy I let up my shirt. How could he do this to me?

Before I know it, I've leaped out of my chair and smacked him as hard as I can across his face. Someone grabs my arms from behind. Chilly keeps laughing. Mrs. Sayers shouts, "Audrey! What is going on here? What is going on?"

I'm sent to the office. You can't have girls hauling off and smacking guys around. No, that is not done. Could set a bad precedent. Could be lousy for morale.

"Audrey, I'm surprised," says Mr. Zwieback, the vice principal.

I look at my feet. *Of course you're surprised,* I want to say. *You have the name of a cracker they give to babies.* "I'm surprised, too," I tell him.

"Can you tell me why you decided to hit Mr. Chillman in study period?"

Well, gee, uh, I wanted to wait until lunch, but I was all booked up. "I don't know. He made me mad."

"Does this have anything to do with a certain picture that's been making the rounds?"

"What?" I say. Mr. Zwieback's seen the picture? *Mr. Zwieback?* Mr. Zwieback has a basset-hound face and long sideburns—no, not the cool kind. He wears plaid—also not the cool kind. Mr. Zwieback grew up somewhere in the South and occasionally says "y'all." It's impossible that he's seen the picture. Impossible.

A red flush creeps up Mr. Zweiback's neck. "Several copies were found on the computers in the library, though we had trouble identifying the, uh, subjects. But your father did call me to discuss the picture," he says. "He told me that it's been sent from student to student. He was quite upset."

I close my eyes and hope for death.

Mr. Zwieback clears his throat. "I understand that something like that could make you angry. I would be angry. Now, if you're sure that Mr. Chillman was, uh, involved in the situation somehow, I can talk to him. I can make sure he's punished for it."

Of course I want to punish him. I want him drawn and quartered. I want him burned at the stake. But if I make a bigger deal of this, then everyone will be reminded all over again. I don't want any more copies of that picture pasted to my locker or in my e-mail box or on my phone. I want it over. "Chilly likes harassing me. He's been doing it forever. I got sick of it."

"I don't want to embarrass you, but I promised your father I would keep an eye out for any trouble. If someone at this school has victimized you or forced you—"

A lightning strike would be perfect right about now. A massive mudslide. A stampede of zebras. "Nobody forced me to do anything, Mr. Zwieback."

Mr. Zwieback frowns, as if he has no idea what to make of this. Of course I was victimized, of course I was forced. Nice girls are forced, honors students are forced. If I wasn't forced . . .

He taps a pen methodically on the top of his desk, *tap, tap, tap.* "Several of the teachers and administrators were in favor of taking action against you."

I'm so surprised that my eyeballs almost pop from my face. "What? What do you mean?"

"I'm not saying I agree with them, but some people feel that our top students should set a better example."

I can't speak. *I* should set a better example, but not Luke. No, that boy's obviously doing just dandy as he is. It's those girls that you have to watch. Girls are tricky. I see Mr. Zwieback eyeing my hair and I wonder what he thinks of the dye job, if he thinks that I tried to change the inside by changing the outside, the way that other kids do. But my inside had already changed, had gone odd and dark somehow. All I did was match it. I stare at Mr. Zwieback until he looks down at his desk.

"Well," he says. "Since we couldn't be absolutely positive who was in the photo, we could hardly take action. That wouldn't be fair." Mr. Zwieback clears his throat. "In any case, I'm sure you understand that you can't go around hitting people."

"Yes," I say. My voice is so low I can hardly hear it myself.

"Normally, something like this would be an automatic suspension. Considering the circumstances, however, and the fact that you've never been in trouble before, I'm going to let you off with a detention."

I can't say *thank you* so I say "Fine."

"I will tell Mr. Chillman to stay far away from you. And I want you to stay away from him, do you understand? No talking, no arguing, and absolutely no hitting."

"It will be hard to avoid him. He sits next to me in history and in study."

"As of today, he does not. I'll inform your teachers." He meets my eyes. "I don't see the need to call your parents, so I won't."

At this, I do say "Thanks."

"Audrey," says Mr. Zwieback, placing his pen carefully on his desk as if it were made of something very fragile, like plastic explosive. "I understand that sometimes young people get a little overwhelmed and do things that they regret later."

"Uh-huh," I say.

"Maybe that's the situation here? Did you want to talk to the school counselor about it?"

The school counselor, Ms. Jones, is having a not-so-secret affair with Mr. Kinsey, the Honors Physics teacher. They'd been spotted coming out of the lab looking dazed and disheveled, as if they'd just performed some complicated experiments with combustible materials.

"No, I don't need to talk to the counselor."

"It could help," he says. "Maybe we could do something for you."

"I'm okay," I say.

He sighs, sees that he's been beaten. "No more hitting?"

My new hair and this whole drama has made me feel as if my world has tilted off its axis. I don't know how Joelle can stand to live like this all the time. "No more hitting," I say.

"Good," he says. "You're a wonderful student, Audrey. I really don't want you to take a bad turn here."

I stand up to go. "Me neither."

Pay Up

"So much for a disguise," says Ash. "Everyone's talking about you again."

We're sitting in the cafeteria, waiting for Joelle.

"Yeah, well. . . ," I say. I'm ignoring all the stares and pointing. Let them point. Let them stare. I see Cindy Terlizzi and Pam Markovitz huddled at the corner table, and I wave cheerily at them.

"I'm going to call you 'slugger' from now on. I'm going to call you 'gangsta girl.'" Ash whips out a mirror and reapplies a thick ring of dark blue eyeliner around each eye. "I can't believe it took you this long to hit that stupid Chilly. You should have smacked him, like, two years ago." She tosses her mirror and liner into her backpack.

"I was gearing up for it," I say.

"I hope you broke his face," she says.

"Don't think so, but we can keep our fingers crossed."

"Remember how pissed off he was when you dumped him? Remember how he called you all the time? Followed you around and stuff? God, what a freaking loser."

"Yeah, and I'm the freaking loser that actually went out with him. Ugh." I shivered.

"Did he actually admit he took the picture and sent it around?"

"He didn't deny it."

"*Arschloch.*"

Joelle flies into the cafeteria, flapping her arms like a bird. "Tayari told me what happened!" she says, throwing her purse up on the table. "Are you all right?"

"I'm fine, Jo," I tell her. "He didn't hit me, I hit him."

"I love it!" she squeals. "If you hadn't done it—"

"You would have shoved your boot down his throat," Ash and me finished for her.

"Exactly," Joelle says. She thrusts her hands into my hair. "Audrey, I can't stop telling you how much this rocks! Are you going to get highlights on top? Or bangs? Bangs would look great on you! But you need to wear more eye makeup. Ash, why don't you give her some of your eyeliner?"

"Yes, Master," Ash says. Her eyes dart behind me and I turn to look. Luke and Nardo stand in the doorway of the cafeteria, talking to two junior girls. Luke sees me and his mouth stops moving for a second; I can tell that he's surprised by the hair. It's the first time in a week that he's looked at me with anything other than a total granite face.

"I guess we know now that Luke didn't have anything to do with that picture," I say.

"But he's still acting like it's *your* fault, like you did something to him," says Joelle. "Ignoring you and whatever. Where does he get off? Oh!" she says, when she realizes the pun. There's no escaping all the sex puns—they're everywhere.

"Forget about him, Audrey," Ash says quietly. "It's not worth getting upset about. I think he's already moved on."

I nod and pick at my fingernails. Joelle pats my elbow and shoots Luke a glare that could shatter glass.

"Look at him," says Joelle. "He was in that picture, too, but he gets to stand there, all proud of himself.

Probably thinks the whole world is lining up to blow him."

I rub my temples. "They pretty much are, aren't they?"

"It's a good thing that's all you did," Joelle says. "Think about how much worse it could be."

They don't know how much worse it is. They don't know because I never told them. I wanted to pretend it didn't happen. I wanted to delete it like a text message. But there's Luke—walking, talking, being—and it hurts me. We weren't going out, so why does it hurt me? It feels like this earache I had once. I didn't even know I was sick until the pain got so bad I hoped my eardrum would burst already, just to make it stop.

I want to burst now. "I wish it were all I did," I say.

"What?" Ash and Joelle say at once. "What do you mean?"

When I don't answer, Ash says, "You didn't!"

"Wait," says Joelle, "When? At my party?"

"No," I say. "Before that."

"Details!" shrieks Joelle. "I need details!"

But Ash looks ashen. "Before that?" she says.

"Yeah," I say. "I didn't tell you because, well, I don't know why I didn't tell you. I couldn't."

"Why?"

"I just said, I don't know."

"No," Ash says. "Why did you do it?"

"What do you mean, why?" I say. "Why does anyone?"

"But you were just hooking up!"

Her dark eyes are blazing and I'm confused. "Isn't that what hooking up is?"

"You idiot," she says. "I knew it. You're totally in love with him, aren't you?"

"No," I say. "I mean, I don't think so. I don't know," I shake my head. "I'm not sure."

"So you're not sure if you love him, but you screwed him anyway?" She keeps her voice low, but she may as well be screaming at me. Her face is stiff and furious.

"Hey, Ash, lighten up," Joelle says.

"You were hooking up just as much as I was," I say. "More."

"I wasn't screwing them all," she says. "What were you thinking?"

"So she got carried away," Joelle says. "Whatever. It happens. Chill out."

I feel tears pressing behind my eyes. I don't understand what's going on, why Ash is so mad at me. There's something she's not telling me. "You were with Jimmy," I say.

"I loved Jimmy." She spits the word *loved*. "We were going out for more than a year. It's different."

"Oh," I say. It's all I can say. I look down at the table. In the surface, someone has carved a heart with an arrow through it, but the initials inside the heart have worn away.

Ash sighs, and her voice loses its awful jagged edges. "I worry about you. I don't want you to end up like that bitch Cherry. Or like them." She jerks her head at the back table, where Cindy Terlizzi and Pam Markovitz are splitting an enormous plate of cheese fries, dropping the fries into their mouths and licking their fingers.

"It sounds like you think I'm already like them," I say.

"No, I don't. But you have to be careful."

"I was trying."

"You need to try harder."

"Thanks for the advice," I say sarcastically. "How do you know what they're like, anyway?"

Ash folds her arms across her chest. "*Now* what are you talking about?"

"Pam. Cindy. How do we know who they've really been with, who they loved or didn't love? How do you know that Pam Markovitz didn't think she loved Jay Epstein when she gave him head at the movies?"

"That's stretching it," Joelle says.

"Maybe, maybe not." I look at Ash. "You're always saying that we should be like guys, act like guys. Does anyone ask them if they love every person they have sex with? Does anyone even care?"

"Okay," says Joelle. "I think we need to talk about

something else now. Like maybe the *Hamlet* auditions tomorrow."

"Forget it," I say. It's bad enough that the entire school believes I'm some kind of whore, but Ash? *Ash?* Who's known me since forever? Who came over after my first kiss with Albert Mendez because it was so disgusting and I couldn't stop crying and had convinced myself I must be a lesbian? Who called Chilly's mom and told her that her son was stalking me and that he needed therapy? Ash?

It's too much.

"You guys think I'm such a slut, then I guess I should be sitting with the sluts, shouldn't I? I wouldn't want you to get a reputation."

I grab my backpack, throw it up on my shoulder, and march over to the corner table. Cindy and Pam gape as I toss my pack to the floor, slip into one of the seats next to them, and pull a gooey fry from the greasy plate. "Mind if I sit here?" I say to them before popping the fry into my mouth.

Cindy and Pam exchange looks.

"What?" I say.

Holding a pencil like a cigarette between her fingers, Pam considers me.

"What?" I say again.

"What, nothing," Pam says. She flicks her eyes at the plate and shrugs. "Your share's $1.25. Pay up."

Duck-Billed Salad Servers

I have not talked to Ash in four days. Joelle
is trying to help, but she's all distracted by the
Hamlet auditions and subsequent rehearsals. She
shouldn't have worried. She's the only one in the
whole school who could handle this backwards,
too-cool-for-school girl Hamlet: "To be or not to
be—*so* not the question." A guy named Joe, a

tall, sort-of-hot junior we've never met before, is cast as O, the male version of Ophelia. When they have to read together and Joelle shouts "Get thee to a monastery!" right up in his face, O/Joe looks more than a bit frightened, and more than a bit turned on.

Ms. Godwin makes me chief set designer, no shock to me or anyone else. She doesn't want any Venetian canals or medieval throne rooms, but she does want some sort of elaborate contemporary sets that we'll have to put on dollies. I thought that it might cheer me up, but it doesn't. I don't have any urge to start drawing up plans, and I don't feel like issuing any orders to my crew. All my usual set-design minions—geeky, pimpled boys, usually in the lower grades, who have weird geeky crushes on me (worse now that there's that stupid picture floating around)—are disappointed. They want to know why I dyed my hair, they want to know why I don't understand that blondes have more fun or are at least more fun to look at, they want to know if I plan on cutting my hair off, and they threaten to quit if I do. Minions don't like change.

I don't like change, either. My dad usually helps me with my drawings, usually takes me to pick up materials. I don't even want to ask him. He's so weird around me now, like a feral cat or something, all jumpy and ready to spit. He works even more, if that's possible, and when he's not working at the store, he's working at home, doing paperwork or housework or stupid projects that keep him from having to see me. When I find him building a bookcase in the basement, I offer to tack it for him—that is, dust it with a tack cloth before he applies the finish. Gruffly, he says, "No, no, I'm fine. Don't want you to get all dirty." I've gone from being his honorary son—the fill-in for Henry, the real boy that should have lived to stand by his dad's side—to this funky GIRL who does icky GIRL things that men—okay, fathers—can't deal with. And I can't deal with it, either.

"When is Dad going to start treating me like a person again?" I ask my mom on the way to the dreaded gynecologist's appointment. I ask because I want to know, and also because I want to distract myself from the Ash disaster and from the stupid appointment. My stomach is hiding in my esophagus, and all of my other organs have switched places. I hate doctors, every kind of doctor. I hate their white coats and weird smiles and rubber gloves and sticks and needles and blank faces. I decide that if I ever have to give birth, I'm going to squat in a field like my ancestors did.

"You have to give Dad a little more time, Audrey," my mom says. "He wasn't prepared for this."

"He must have assumed that I would have a boyfriend at some point in my life."

"Yes," says my mom, with a glance at me, "but no one assumed that you would be photographed in a compromising position with said boyfriend when you were only sixteen years old."

"I'll be seventeen soon."

"And," she continues, "no one assumed that the compromising photograph would be spread around cell phones and on the Internet." She's breathing sharply through her nose, so I can tell she's annoyed and upset with me for being all ha-ha about it. "At least you can't see your face. It seems like this photograph won't haunt you forever."

"That doesn't seem to make Dad feel any better."

"To tell you the truth, it doesn't make me feel much better, either, and I'm not sure if you should feel better. What's going on with you today?"

"Nothing," I say. "I just don't want to think about it the rest of my life. I don't think that's such a bad thing." This is not the way I really feel about it, but I'm trying. I change the subject. "How's the new book coming?"

"Fine," she says. Another sideways glance. "I've just introduced a new character, a delinquent teenage girl who drives everyone crazy. She chokes on an oatmeal-raisin muffin and has to be given the Heimlich."

"Great."

The doctor's office looks like all doctor's offices: that is, it's got the white walls, the bad art, and the *People* magazines everywhere. I have to spend forever filling out endless medical history forms with questions about whether my great-great-great-great-great-great-grandmother ever had a stroke, or maybe a hangnail. Finally some nurse comes to get me. After I get weighed and blood-pressured, I have to get naked, put on this little paper cape that ties in the front and a teeny paper blankie over my lap, and sit shivering in a freezing office. Who thinks this stuff up?

There's a knock on the door, and the doctor marches in. He's followed by the nurse who took my blood pressure, a grumpy woman who looks like a giant potato with legs.

"Hello, Audrey. I'm Dr. Warren," he says. "You already met Nurse Thrane."

"Hi," I say. He shakes my hand and I check him out. Dark, balding dad type. I decide that this is better than a blond, not-balding hot type, at least when it comes to gynecologists.

He pulls up a black stool and sits. "So it looks like we're going to do a general exam today."

"Great!" I say, weirdly. "I mean, fine."

"Looks like your blood pressure is good. Any trouble with headaches?"

I shrug. "Not really. If I haven't had enough sleep or if I have a cold or whatever, sometimes my head hurts a little."

"Have you ever had a migraine? A severe headache?"

"No. Never."

"Any relatives with migraines?"

"I don't think so."

"Problems with menstrual pain? Cramps? Back-aches?"

"No."

He scribbles something in a file folder.

"Any problems with your breasts?"

Like what? Having them sneak out at night? "No."

"Are you sexually active, Audrey?"

Sigh. "I was."

He doesn't look up from the chart. "And when was that?"

"About a month ago."

"This is intercourse? About a month ago?"

"Yes," I say.

"Birth control?"

"I . . . he . . . we used a condom."

"Have you ever been pregnant, or are you concerned that you're pregnant now?"

To quote Ash: Jesus! "No," I say.

"When was your last period?"

"Uh . . ." I mentally count the days. "Two weeks ago?"

"And how many sexual partners have you had?"

Oh, thousands. "One."

"Okay." He stands and goes to the sink to wash his hands. While he's lathering up, he says, "I'm going to

140

check your breasts first." He dries his hands and then slaps them together, rubbing them, I suppose, to warm them up. Then he slips underneath the paper thingy I'm wearing with his scratchy fingers, and presses all around my boobs—quite possibly the strangest medical thing that's ever been done to me. The nurse watches, yawning.

"Everything's the way it's supposed to be," he says. He pulls two rubber gloves out of a box on the counter and puts them on. They're exactly the same brand of glove, I see, that I bought at the beauty supply store. This seems all wrong to me.

"Now I want you to lie back on the table and put your feet in these stirrups."

Put my feet up in what? Are you freaking kidding me? I do what he says, though, focusing hard on the ceiling. It's one of those white cork ceilings with all the crazy pockmarks. "Audrey, I need you to open your knees."

"Sorry," I say. I'm blushing, but the nurse still looks bored as she hands the doctor what looks like a huge plastic salad server shaped like a duck's bill.

"This is a speculum, Audrey," he says. "I'm going to insert this and get a better look at your cervix, okay? You might feel a bit of pressure." I feel something poking at me. "Audrey, try and relax."

YOU RELAX!!! I take a deep breath. The salad server forces its way in. It doesn't hurt, exactly, but it's weird and I hate it. "Ow," I say.

"Are you okay?" he says.

No. "I guess."

"You're doing great, Audrey." He looks around inside me for a while. "I'm going to take a swab of your vaginal secretions."

Ew. "What for?" I say.

"Just to make sure there's no infection. It's routine."

Infection. Right. How nice.

He pokes around some more. "Everything is looking healthy, Audrey. I'm going to remove the speculum now. Then I'm going to insert two fingers to check your ovaries and fallopian tubes, all right?"

NO! NO! NO! "All right."

He stands and sticks his fingers inside me while pressing down on my stomach from the outside. He looks thoughtfully off into the air as he does this, as if he's composing poetry or writing songs in his head. I think he's a terrible person. Only sick and terrible people would want to do this for a living.

"Okay," he says. He pulls his fingers out and whips off the gloves while Nurse Potato adjusts the stirrups and helps me to sit up again. "Though we'll make sure of it with some tests, everything looks fine to me."

Exhale. "I'm glad," I say.

He plunks down on his trusty black stool. "Now, since you are sexually active, I do want to talk to you about a couple of things. You told me that you used a condom, and that's good. Condoms can do a lot to protect you from a whole host of sexually transmitted diseases like chlamydia, gonorrhea, HIV, and genital warts."

"Warts," I say. "I don't like the sound of warts." My hands twist in my lap, crinkling the paper blankie. I know about warts and about a lot of other stuff, mostly from books and the Internet, but also from Mrs. Hurtado, our ninth-grade Sex Ed teacher. Mrs. Hurtado was fearless. She showed us a movie of a live birth that looked so bloody and painful it had every girl surrounding her desk afterward, carefully examining all the methods of birth control she'd brought with her. She would answer any question we had with complete seriousness, no matter how dumb, like *Isn't birth control the girl's job?* or, *You can't get pregnant your first time, right?*

"Warts are one thing," the doctor is saying. "But there's also some evidence that condoms might offer protection against something called HPV, human papillomavirus, that can cause cervical cancer down the road if it's untreated. I want you to keep using condoms, Audrey, whenever you have sex. Nonlubricated condoms for oral sex, too. And I want you to have regular checkups."

He makes it sound as if I were having sex every other

day. I'm not sure I'll ever have sex again. "Okay," I say.

"Now, condoms are fairly effective in deterring pregnancy, up to ninety-seven percent. But only if they're used correctly. Make sure you read the package yourself; don't leave it up to your partner to figure everything out. And I'd recommend another form of birth control for you to use in conjunction with condoms. You're young and healthy, so I think the birth control pill would be an excellent choice. You can also consider Depo-Provera shots. Ninety-nine point seven percent effective."

Shots? I need shots? "I don't want shots," I say.

He smiles at me, a bland, just-giving-you-the-facts smile. "You don't have to get shots. You don't have to get anything. But I do want you to remember that no single birth control method is one hundred percent effective, okay? Not condoms, not pills, not anything. Only total abstinence works all the time."

Duh. "I know."

"So then you can understand why we think it's a good idea for you to select a birth control method to prevent pregnancy and pair that with condoms to prevent STDs."

"Yes," I say.

"The nurse will give you some information to take home, and you can think about it. Are your parents with you?"

"My mom is here."

"Then maybe you can discuss it with her to come up with the best option for you."

"Okay," I say. Now I think he's terrible *and* insane.

"Do you have any questions?"

Yeah, when can I get out of here? "I don't think so," I say.

"If you have any problems or any questions, I want you to call me right away. We'll be happy to help you." He smiles again, this time in a friendly and sort of fatherly way, and he doesn't seem so terrible. "We'll leave you to get dressed now. The nurse will be back in a few minutes to take you to the waiting room. Remember, you can come back or call at any time if you want to discuss birth control options or if anything else comes up. Other than that, I'd like to see you in a year for a checkup."

"Okay," I say.

"Good." He shakes my hand one last time, and then he and Nurse Potato are out the door. I rip off the flimsy outfit and throw on my clothes. My head is spinning with visions of condoms and warts, swabs and shots. When the nurse takes me back to the waiting room and I see my mother sitting there and I hear her murmur "How was it?" I realize something. If every teenager had to have this exam, if guys had to have some giant duck-billed salad server shoved up their butts on a regular basis, if every high schooler had to hear the words

WARTS and GENITALS and CANCER in the same freaking conversation while wearing nothing but a couple of napkins, no one would ever have sex again, and that could be the whole point.

The Slut City World Tour

When I sat down with Pam Markovitz and Cindy Terlizzi and sampled their fries, I never thought that it would become a habit. But every day, I walk into the lunchroom and see Ash turn from me as if I have human papillomavirus, see Joelle look faint and theatrical. Then I scan the room and see Pam clearing a seat for me. One thing leads to the next, and then I'm sitting with them all the time.

At first we don't talk much. We order cheese fries, split them three ways, and eat them, occasionally complaining about a teacher or some stupid guy who said some stupid thing. I tell them that Ash thinks I'm a slut and I don't want to hang out with her, and they don't ask for the gory details.

We start to talk. Things that I didn't know about Pam Markovitz: (a) she's funny; (b) she's smarter than everyone thinks she is; and (c) she's sworn off guys. She says she's had enough of them to know that they just aren't worth it, at least not at this age. "Do you know that the last guy I went out with was trying to get in my pants in the car on the way to the movies? He didn't even wait for me to get my seat belt on, just 'Hey, how are you, you look nice,' and wham! right for the fly. I'm like, Whoa! And he's like, What? As if normal people always ram their hands down each other's pants on first dates." She waves the air in front of her face as if there's a cloud of smoke, which of course there isn't, because we're in school. "I'm not wasting any more time with *boys*. What do they know about pleasing a girl?" she says. "Nothing. That's what they know. I'm saving myself for a man."

"Seems like a good plan to me," I say.

She nods at me. "You get it. You found out the hard

way. Heh. No pun intended."

It's the first time they've said anything about the picture or about Luke. I'm tempted to ask Pam if she was with him, too, but I don't, because I know she was and because I really don't want to hear about it. "Yeah," I say. "I found out the hard way." And, to be mean, because I am feeling mean lately, I say, "Or the not-so-hard way."

"The never-hard-enough way!" says Cindy. She laughs, open-mouthed, and then covers her mouth with her hand. Cindy's bottom teeth are crooked, and she's really self-conscious about them. Pam told me that the first thing Cindy wants to do when she turns eighteen is to audition for *Extreme Makeover* or one of those other plastic surgery shows, like maybe something on MTV. She wants the works: teeth, boobs, cheeks, other cheeks, etc. I think that those shows make everyone look like the talking robots at Epcot Center, but what's the point of telling her that? People don't listen.

"You guys should try Pam's Boy-Free Plan," Pam says. "I feel great. No hassles, no stupid phone calls at midnight, no begging. No telling me that rubbers ruin the sex for them. Poor, poor babies. Please. Give me a break." She glares out the window, as if the boys who said these things to her are chained up outside, just waiting for her to come and kick the crap out of them for fun.

"I think things used to be better for women," Cindy says. "I'm reading this book where this woman gets kidnapped and has to be harem girl for this guy?"

"Which book is this?" I say.

Cindy digs around in her bag and pulls it out. The woman on the cover is wearing gauzy, see-through pants and a spangly bra. A guy with long, windblown hair and a windblown white shirt stands behind her, pulling her elbows back in a way that could not be comfortable. The book is called *Slave to Love*.

"Oh, yeah," says Pam. "She looks like she's having a great time. Is he trying to dislocate her shoulders?"

"You didn't let me finish!" says Cindy. "This girl? Her name is Vienna? She gets rescued from the harem by this guy, Rafe, before anything bad happens to her at the harem. And then Rafe falls in love with her. I'm just at the part where he asks her to marry him."

"Sweet," says Pam. "And?"

"What I'm trying to say is that guys used to be gentlemen, didn't they? Some of them, anyway."

"Cindy," I say, "I don't think that those romance novels are historically accurate."

Pam bites the tip off a fry. "Plus, they're rotting your brain."

"Uh-oh," says Cindy, lowering her voice to a hiss. "Don't look now, Audrey, but here comes your little friend. And your other little friend."

I look up and see Ash stomping toward the table, Joelle right behind her. Joelle has a pleading look on her face, like, *Please, don't blame me, I couldn't stop her, you know how she gets*. I do know how Ash gets, but I don't know how she got this way this time. It's been two and a half weeks since our fight. I broke down and called her right after it happened, but she was furious and wouldn't budge. You screwed up, she told me, you need to admit it. I got mad all over again, hung up the phone, buried my face in Stevie's fur. My mom wanted to know why I needed a ride to school all the time, and I made something up about before-school play rehearsals. To keep my mind off the whole thing, I studied even harder. When I aced my latest essay test (*Pride and Prejudice*, 101 percent) Mr. Lambright pulled me aside and told me that whatever I was doing, it was working. Ron the Valedictorian folded his own test (98 percent) and gave me a dirty look.

Now Ash stands next to the table, glaring at me, at us.

"Welcome to Slut City," says Pam, her voice like a refrigerator. "What do *you* want?"

Ash doesn't answer. Her face relaxes, and she flicks at her eyebrow ring nervously. She sighs and stares at the floor. "I've been a jerk."

"Yes," I say. "You have."

"Yeah," says Pam. "You have."

"Ditto," Cindy says.

Nobody breathes for a minute. Then Pam crosses her arms over her chest. "That's it? That's all you're going to say?"

The muscles in Ash's jaw grind and shift, and I'm afraid she's going to tell Pam to screw herself. They have completely different styles and attitudes, but the same sort of fierceness. Inside the rings of liner and shadow, their eyes sparkle with hostility. But instead of telling Pam off, Ash says, "No, that's not all I'm going to say, as if it's any of your business. Audrey, this is all my fault. I just didn't want you to get hurt like I got hurt. And I was upset that you didn't tell me the whole story. But I shouldn't have yelled at you. I'm sorry."

Pam and Cindy glance at me. I know there's more to it, and she owes me, but I can't stay mad. I miss her. "That's okay," I say.

Pam sighs and Cindy shrugs, as if to say, *Oh, well, I guess that's the end of this little friendship, see ya*. But Joelle claps her hands together in relief. "Thank GOD that's over. I was so stressed I thought I would have to get a prescription." She climbs into a seat next to Cindy. "Can I have a fry?"

Just like that, it's the five of us. I don't have to ask my dad to help me get the materials for the *Hamlet* stage set; Cindy's dad has an oversized van. Over

Thanksgiving break, she drives me over to the Home Depot to buy wood, paint, and other supplies. Ash, Pam, and Joelle insist on coming. Pam is a bad influence on Ash; there's enough chain-smoking to fill the entire van with a thick gray cloud. I roll down the windows to let some out. We're like a traveling five-alarm fire.

"Do the two of you have to smoke at the same time?" Joelle says.

Ash and Pam say "Yes."

"I'm freezing, and my clothes are starting to stink," Cindy says. "Smoking is so gross. I don't know how you guys can do it."

Pam says, "You and Joelle could have stayed home."

"I'm not even sure there's going to be enough room for the wood with all of us in the car," I say, my eyes stinging.

"You would have missed me too much if I didn't come with you!" says Joelle.

"Didn't you have a rehearsal or something?" Pam asks her.

"Yes," Joelle says irritably. "But it was only Polonius. I can't stand Polonius."

"Joelle's got a crush on Ophelia," I explain.

"You have a crush on a chick?" says Pam. "That's kind of cool."

"It's O, not Ophelia," Joelle says. "And he's not a

chick. He's a guy. And he's hot."

"Guys, schmuys," Pam says.

It's Cindy's turn to explain: "Pam's sworn off the male species."

"Really?" says Ash, blowing smoke out of her nose, like a cartoon bull.

We park the van and stumble into the store. "Watch this," says Pam. She takes my list, picks out the cutest guy in the lumber department, and goes to work. "Hi," she says, in her honey-gravel voice, "I was wondering if we could—oops!" She drops the list on the floor. She turns away from him, bends from the waist, and picks up the paper. She's wearing a skirt, and the visual is just short of porn. "Sorry," she says sheepishly when she stands up again.

"That's okay," the guy says. You can see the Adam's apple go up and down a few times as he tries to swallow.

"We just need a little help finding all these things, and we're not sure where to look," she says. "Can you help us?" She hands him the list and leans over so that her breasts push up against his arm. His eyes are wide, and he stammers, "Uh, sure. This way." The lumber guy takes us up and down the aisles, pointing out this wood and that wood and grinning like an idiot whenever Pam smiles. He gets us what we need and has it loaded onto a cart by three more grinning idiots in orange aprons, all moving so fast that they're practically blurred. *"Three blind mice*," whispers Ash. "*See how they run.*" Pam thanks the cute guy for all his help by giving his butt a swift pat, turning tail, and leaving him in the dust. As we walk away, we hear him squeaking, "Wait, can I have your number? Wait!"

"Nice," says Ash when we are in the paint department.

"Oh, I could do *that*," Joelle says.

"Any girl can do it," says Pam. "That's the point."

I snort. "And they say girls are easy. Girls are the sluts."

"And we're the biggest sluts of all," Pam says. "Well, except for Cindy."

"What do you mean?" Ash says. Then her eyes widen. "Are you still a virgin?"

A man and a woman wearing matching shirts stop comparing cans of ceiling paint to gape at us.

"Shhh!" Cindy says. "Don't say it so loud."

"I didn't," says Ash.

"And don't look so surprised, either."

"I'm not surprised."

"Yes, you are," Cindy says. She twirls a lock of over-dyed, overfried hair around her finger. "I don't know what the big deal is. Lots of people are virgins. I want to do it with someone I love. Is that such a bad thing?"

I shuffle my feet and will not look at Ash. "No, I think that's a good thing."

"Someday her prince will come," says Pam sarcastically.

"Sure, tons of *those* around," Ash says.

Cindy looks wounded. "I like guys. Just because you hate them doesn't mean that I have to."

"Of course it doesn't," Joelle says, putting her arm around Cindy's shoulders. "Don't let the mean girls bother you. They're dried-up, bitter old hags. Princes don't like bitter old hags. They like nice girls like us."

Ash jerks her head at Joelle. "She's a virgin, too."

"*You?*" Pam and Cindy shout at once. "Get out!"

Smiling proudly, Joelle tosses her head. "Out."

"But you're an actress," Cindy says.

Joelle stamps her foot. "Now, what's *that* supposed to mean? Everyone always *assumes* . . ." She sees the matchy couple sneaking glances at us. "Oh, hello," she says. "Don't mind us. We're rehearsing a scene for a new movie."

"Yeah," says Ash. "It's called *The Slut City World Tour*. Want tickets?"

As if his wife might get ideas, the man drags her away from us by the arm. Pam snickers and Cindy gets nearly hysterical, she thinks it's so funny. It takes more than two hours to buy six cans of paint, a package of screws, ten hinges, and a few doorknobs because Joelle won't stop singing, "*The girls are pretty in Slut City*" and "*In Slut City you won't get no pity*," which she accompanies with high kicks and semi-spastic tap dancing.

Pam shakes a box of nails and holds it up to her ears like a seashell. "I wouldn't mind boys so much if they knew how to give a girl an orgasm."

Ash agrees. "They should offer anatomy lessons at school as a public service."

"I'm not sure it would help," says Cindy, shaking her head gravely. "Boys have concentration problems."

Pam replaces the box of nails. "Ash, you went out with that guitar guy, what's his name, for a while, right? The one in the band?"

"Jimmy," Ash says, looking like someone just poured vinegar into her mouth.

"So was he any good?"

"Good at playing the guitar?"

"Good at sex."

Ash flushes sweetheart pink. "Yeah, he was."

"Really?" Pam says. "How good?"

"Good," says Ash. And I know it's true. Not because she was so free with the details, but because she always had this little smile after she'd been with Jimmy, this sweet, private smile. I wonder how Jimmy could have done it, how he could have made Ash smile like she was keeping the best sort of secret and then leave her without looking back.

Pam's not finished with her questions. "So we're talking orgasms on a regular basis?"

Ash squirms. "Jesus!"

"Pam gets in everyone's business," Cindy says. "She'll talk about anything."

"I'm eighteen years old," Pam says. "I'm a legal adult, and I'll talk about adult things if I want to."

Ash is biting her lip. "With our clothes on," she says.

"Huh?" I say.

Even redder now, Ash says, "If we kept our clothes on, then I would, you know. Something about the pressure . . ."

Joelle shivers. "Orgasms are so cool. You feel nice all over."

Pam's laughter hangs in the air. "Honey, a *cookie* makes you feel nice all over. You probably haven't had an orgasm yet."

"I haven't?" says Joelle, and frowns. "Oh. Well, that sucks."

"A lot of girls don't," says Pam.

"That *really* sucks," Joelle says. "How is that fair?"

"You can always take care of it by yourself, you know," Pam tells her. "Do you have a shower massage?"

"Ew!" Joelle says.

I'm still confused about Ash. "With your clothes *on*?"

Pam shakes her head at my stupidity. To Ash, she says, "With guys, it's so easy. Not so easy for us. And it's not like you get any actual help from *them*. Sometimes

I'd just give up and blow the guy. You can keep your clothes on for *that*. You can wear a winter coat and they don't care." She's dropped the honey out of her honey-gravel voice but seems sad somehow, or maybe disappointed. She sounds like some old barfly talking about her tragic, messed-up youth. We don't know what to say.

To change the subject or to cheer her up, Joelle decides to go back to her high-kick song-and-dance routine, this time singing, *"Here a ho, there a ho, everywhere a ho, ho."* A couple of goons in flannel—one short and light, the other tall and brown—amble by, smirking like fools. "You girls want any help?"

"Why?" says Ash sharply. "You work here?"

"No," said the light one. "But I'm sure I can find whatever it is you need." The brown one laughs.

Joelle turns on her sexiest smile and runs her finger down the light one's chest. "And what do you think we need?"

He jumps a little, as if Joelle's finger were electrified. "Well, uh, I don't know."

"You don't know?" says Joelle. She turns to us. "Girls, did you hear that? They don't know what we need."

Ash elbows Pam, and Pam's back to her smirking, sassy self, a forty-year-old divorcee on a hip TV show. "They don't know what we need?" Pam says. "Now, there's a freaking surprise."

The Third Time
(and Fourth and Fifth and ...)

 arly September, and this was what I needed:

Luke, Luke, and more Luke. School started, and

we passed each other in the hallways. My throat

closed up as if I had some wicked allergy. He said,

"Hey," and I couldn't speak, so I flashed my teeth

in what I hoped was a brilliant smile but was

afraid was the grimace of a constipated baboon.

"You avoiding me?" he said at the first party after school started, at Ray Dale's house on the second Saturday of the month. I wasn't big on parties during the school year, but I had been frantic to go to this one because I thought I'd see Luke there. I did, but he had to torture me first. For close to an hour, me and Ash watched him make the rounds, flirting with every girl in the place. Nearly puking with anxiety, I was digging around in the fridge for something nonalcoholic to drink when he spoke.

"What?" I said. I dropped a can of Pepsi on my foot. "Ow!"

"Are you okay?"

I winced. "Yeah, I'm fine."

Ash, who was leaning against the kitchen counter, said, "Hey, Luke."

Luke turned. "Oh, sorry, Ash. Didn't see you. What's up?"

"Not much," she said, giving him her own monkey grimace. She nodded at me. "I'll be in the other room."

Luke called after her, "Nardo's in the basement."

"Yeah," Ash said. "Thanks."

Luke turned back to me. "So," he said.

"So." My foot was killing me. I held it up, like a bear with a thorn in its paw.

Luke grabbed a bunch of paper towels off the roll hanging from the wall and wrapped some ice in them.

"Sit," he told me, pushing me into one of the kitchen chairs. He pulled up another chair and placed my foot between his knees. After sliding off my flip-flop, he pressed the ice to my foot. "Better?"

"Yeah." And not because of the ice, either. He seemed to have some sort of foot fetish. Not that I minded.

He held the ice on my foot for a few minutes. "So you're not avoiding me?"

"No," I said. I thought it was a retarded question, especially after the marathon flirting he'd been doing at the party. "Why would you think that?"

He peeked up at me. "I don't know. I must be nervous around you or something."

This made me laugh. "That must be it."

Luke pulled the ice away from my foot. "I think you're going to live."

I didn't know what it was, but just being near him sometimes turned me into a completely different person, this say-anything person. It was a person I wanted to be, but also a person I was afraid of. If she'd *say* anything, what would she *do*?

"Are you sure it's all right?" I said. "I might need more medical attention."

"Medical attention," he said, pulling a shifty little grin. "I don't think you need me for that. You're a genius, right? You can probably diagnose and treat yourself."

And then, sometimes, I'd come rushing back to myself—the tense Audrey, the hyper Audrey. "Shut up," I said. I'd meant for it to sound teasing and sexy, but it came out whiny and annoyed. I was tired of everyone getting on my case for the work I did.

"Sorry," he said. "I was just joking."

"I know. I'm just . . . Look, I'm no genius, okay?"

He paused. "You did skip a couple of grades."

"One grade. *Third* grade. And not because I'm smarter than everyone else. Only cause I'm a finisher."

"A finisher," he said. "Sounds like the title of a kung fu movie. *The Finisher*." He punched the air.

"It wouldn't make a very good movie." For some reason, I felt like I should explain it to him. "Like, you get an assignment in English class to read five chapters in whatever book. How many times do you actually read all five of them when you're supposed to?"

"People *read* books? That's so strange. I thought they were just decoration."

"Ha-ha," I said.

"I've been known to read the occasional book," he told me. "I finished *Moby Dick*. Funny."

"You thought *Moby Dick* was *funny*?"

"Yeah. Mostly, though, I skim. I'm more of a skimmer." The tips of his fingers skimming up my calf demonstrated his skills.

Moby Dick should have distracted me, the skimming

should have distracted me, but I was in Audrey Overthink mode and there was no stopping me. "I read all my chapters," I said. "Every word. Twice, or maybe three times. Every assignment I get, I finish as fast as I can. Papers, homework, posters, essay tests, whatever. If the rest of you guys finished everything you were supposed to *when* you were supposed to, you would have skipped grades, too."

"Come on. You've never blown off a homework assignment? Or a chapter? Not once?"

"No," I said. "When I was in kindergarten, the first day, we got this purple workbook, right? With all these little exercises in it, spelling and colors and that kind of thing. And I was so excited that I sat down and finished the entire book, beginning to end, then and there. I thought my teacher was going to have a heart attack when I showed her."

"I feel one coming on now," Luke said.

"It's like I can't *not* finish," I said. "I don't know why." Which was a lie. I knew why. If I didn't study as hard as I could for a test, I could fail. And if I failed one test, I could fail two. If I failed two, I could fail them all. And if I failed them all, then I wouldn't go to college. And if I couldn't go to college, I couldn't study architecture or design or anything else, and my life would be ruined. Because of the one test I didn't study for, the one chapter I didn't read. That's all it takes. One mistake, and everything you've worked for is gone. It happens all the time. It happened to my parents. I came along and blasted everything to pieces. Instead of a graduate degree for my mom and a law degree for my dad, they did the right thing and had a wedding. And they didn't even get the baby brother to complete the family portrait.

Luke said nothing for a few minutes, and I figured that I'd ruined the mood with this lecture on my deranged study habits. Who the hell wants to talk about kindergarten workbooks? Sex-y.

Luke stood and pulled me to my feet, or foot, because I couldn't put any real weight on my right one.

"This really hurts," I said. "Who knew Pepsi cans were so deadly?"

"Here," he said. "Let me help you." He tossed the wet wad of paper towels in the sink and swung me up into his arms, which was totally terrifying because he's not that big and I'm not that small.

"You've *got* to be kidding," I said as he carried me toward the stairs. On the way, we passed Ray Dale, who raised his fist in the air and said, "Dude! Caveman!"

"You're not going to drop me, are you?" I said as Luke took the stairs.

"You doubt my animal strength?"

"No, I don't," I said, "but I also don't doubt my animal weight."

"You're as light as a feather. Actually, you're lighter

than a feather. You're like a mote of dust."

"That's romantic," I said.

He kicked open the door of one of the bedrooms and tossed me on the bed. It was a twin, which made things cozy when he jumped up on the bed, too. I tried to keep breathing. It was a struggle.

"I missed you," he said. He cupped my chin with his hand and kissed me, hard and deep and twisty-twirly. My mind turned into Luke's little mote of dust. An angry, stompy little mote that wanted his shirt off NOW, IMMEDIATELY; that found shirts unnecessary and absolutely, utterly criminal. I pawed at his T-shirt, and let out a strangled mewl as he yanked it off. The sight of him, lean and rippled, threatened to unknit my skin. It didn't take long for his hand to slip inside my top, his fingers tracing my ribs.

"Your bones are so cool," he said.

"Huh?" I said, kiss-drunk.

He brushed against the lace trim of my bra and crawled under the underwire. Cupping my breast, he squeezed in the most delicious way. I heard myself make a low animal noise somewhere deep in my throat.

He rolled over with me in his arms, so that I was straddling him. He tugged my shirt up around my armpits and had my bra undone about two seconds later. Rubbing our chests and hips and thighs together, we rocked until the bed started creaking like an old wooden boat, until my underwear was drenched and he was groaning like his own bones had spontaneously shattered all at once.

Later, on the way home, Ash asked me sarcastically if I'd had a good time.

"It was okay," I said, brushing my swollen, couch-pillow lips with the back of my hand.

So this is what I became: strangled and mute at school, when I could see but not touch, and a frothing wildebeest at this party and that party, none of which I would have gone to if I didn't think there was a chance that Luke would be there. I'd watch him flirt with the universe and I'd want to die; then he'd come find me and we'd disappear into bedrooms or closets or basements, wherever we could. Ash kept warning me to be cool, to not take things so seriously, to not be surprised that Luke flirted so much. "He's a player and you know it. If he wasn't, he'd be calling you, all right? You'd, like, have a real date or something? But he's not calling you. This is a casual thing, a hookup thing, a friends-with-benefits thing. Don't lose your mind," she said. "If you don't chill, you're going to get hurt."

It wasn't just Ash. I'd walk into a room and the first thing I would get was a report on Luke's whereabouts from people who liked me, glares and sneers from anyone who didn't. After that, we retreated to the only private place left, his mom's van, which he would drive to some dark corner so that no one would show up and peek through the windows. He removed the last bench seat in the back and replaced it with a fluffy old comforter we could roll around on, or roll up in like human enchiladas. We'd jump into the van, shut the door, and fall against each other, falling into each other, going further and further every time we were together.

One night, my top and bra were stripped off and flung into the driver's seat before we even had a chance to kiss. Instead of going for my mouth, Luke started to kiss my breasts instead. My eyes rolled back so far in my head that I thought they were going to keep rolling; I wouldn't be seeing Luke, I'd be seeing the happy thoughtless cloud of my own brain, that bright white pulsing nothing, and it seemed like the very nicest thing that could happen, the sweetest thing, to see your brain.

I covered us with the blanket as he unbuttoned my jeans and eased them off, and I worked him out of his. The two of us were wearing only our underwear, which should have made me stop, which should have made me think, but didn't mean much to me except for the fact that now his hands could go almost anywhere and *were* everywhere and I loved his hands best of all because they had these beautiful fingers that poked me and tickled me, rubbed me and hollowed me out. He tapped the inside of my knee and my legs fell open as if he had just pushed a lever. I couldn't stop them and I didn't want to. *More!* bubbled my bright, cottony brain, *Moremoremoremore,* as his hand danced between my legs. I thought about grabbing it, guiding it, showing him exactly where and how to touch me, but as bold and brave and going-places-I'd-never-gone-before as I was, I wasn't that bold or that brave. My own hands started to travel. He had miles and miles of saltysmooth skin and all of it was mine. I could feel his hard-on burning a brand on my hip, heard the sharp intake of breath when I pressed against it.

He shifted and pulled the blanket off us. I felt the rush of cool air and the pressure of his lips as he kissed his way down my neck, breastbone, and stomach, past my belly button and lower and lower and lower. His fingertips curled into the top of my underwear and started to peel it down my hips. I lost the yummy feeling in my head and my body. My brain got all chattery like it always did, chattery and stupid and judgey: *I want him to feel me but don't want him to see me my boobs are like pancakes and my stomach sticks out and my butt is all squished against the floor and what if I like it and start flailing around or what if I* don't *like it and start flailing around or what if I taste funny and he* doesn't *like it and . . .*

I grabbed his face and hauled him eye level.

"What's the matter?" he said.

"Nothing," I said. "I want you up here."

He looked at me for what felt like a century. "Are you sure?"

"Yes," I said. With all that we'd done, it was dumb to be embarrassed, but I was embarrassed. I felt more naked than naked. I felt like crying.

"Okay. Whatever you want," he said. He stroked my body. "You're pretty."

I wanted to believe him and I sort of believed him, but I reached for the blanket and pulled it back over us.

We lay there for a while, not touching, not talking. Then I felt his hand around my wrist and thought, *Okay, here it comes, he's all mad, he's going to start complaining, he's going to ask me to have sex with him or at least go down on him or something, because he at least TRIED to do it to me and it's only fair.* But all he did was massage my wrist and palm, press my knuckles between his thumb and his index finger.

"Your hands are so small," he said.

My hands always seemed pretty regular to me. "They are?"

"Uh-huh," he said. "They're nice."

Him saying my hands were nice made me feel nice. I took one of my nice hands and put it on his nicer chest. His heart fluttered under my palm. I thought about the ventricles pumping his blood through his veins. And then I thought about the veins themselves, pushing up through the skin on his arms and legs as if they could barely contain the fluid.

I slid my hand down his chest and stomach and then wriggled my fingers in the waistband of his underwear. His breathing went ragged as I brushed the tip of his penis, wrapped my hand around it. I couldn't believe that skin and blood could get so hard.

I squeezed. "Does that hurt?"

His eyes were like pools of motor oil, dark and glazed. "Are you kidding?"

"I'm curious."

"No, it doesn't hurt," he said. "I like it."

I ran my thumb in circles over the tip, where it was plush and sort of spongy. It felt like a warm and fleshy version of a video game control. Luke control. It was cool, but also kind of odd. Like, guys walk around all day with this thing hanging off them, this thing that seemed like it could make you feel really good, insanely good, but also could betray your thoughts or maybe even work against you. What's it like to have this THING?

He closed his eyes. "You're trying to kill me, aren't you?"

My face burned. I didn't know what I was trying to do except maybe drive him crazy. I liked the idea that I could drive him crazy; I wanted to keep doing that. And

I wanted to keep him coming back to me, I wanted to keep him kissing me and touching me and telling me I was pretty. I started to move my hand, hoping I was doing it right. "I am trying to kill you," I said. "But I hope you'll die happy."

A Long, Cold Winter

Once we have the lumber and the supplies, I throw myself into designing the *Hamlet* set. My minions are thrilled to be put to work nailing and building and painting, even more thrilled when I yell at them for not following the drawings I created on my computer (I always feel horrible after I yell, so I buy them corn chips and pizza). I spend my free time—all twenty-two minutes of it—raiding thrift stores for random items: phones, curtains, dishes, chairs, and one human skull. My studying is done between the hours of ten and two every night, and I'm beginning to look like a skull myself.

Because Pam and Cindy have nothing better to do, they visit me on the set every afternoon, teasing the minions mercilessly and making snack and beverage runs to keep us going. Ash hangs out in the back of the auditorium, weeding through bad poetry submissions and pulling out her hair. "Tentacles!" she shrieks at one particularly tense moment. "Why is everyone writing about *tentacles*?!"

The performances are right before Christmas break. In Ms. Godwin's updated, girl-power version of *Hamlet*, Joelle rocks the house, as we all knew she would. She's fierce, she's confused, she's furious, she's sexy, she's murderous, she's sad, she's scared—she's every emotion a person ever had, all packaged up in the body of a pop star. Watching her, I feel this funny feeling, this end-of-life-as-we-know-it feeling. We all thought that Joelle had no plans after graduation except to do more commercials, but Joelle has submitted an application to the drama program at Juilliard and is scheduled to audition in January. When she takes her final bows and someone runs out to give her a bouquet of flowers, I feel like the curtain is coming down on us all, that we've got to start gearing up to leave this school behind. I don't know how I'll make it without seeing Ash and Joelle every day. All I've ever wanted was to be older, to be free, and instead I feel young and lost and stupid. I tell Ash, and she tells me to knock it off. "Months, Aud. We've got months left."

"If you include vacations, it's only four months," I say.

"I keep telling you, the key word is *months*. Now read this and tell me what you think of it. Is the line about the black bile spewing from the dead guy's mouth a little much, or what?"

Christmas comes, and I take Joelle to Christmas Eve services with us just so that she can see what it's like. She freaks over the church—"This is so cool! Like Europe or something!" she says, and really gets into singing the hymns. She promises that she'll take me to temple sometime if I really want to go. There are no pretty stained-glass windows to look at, she says, and there's no Jesus, but she thinks I'll like the rabbis singing in Hebrew. "Just don't expect any Bat Mitzvah, wedding, 'Hava Nagila' stuff. It's not all dancing around with chairs."

Over Christmas vacation, I spend practically every second reading and studying for finals in January. The girls drag me out of the house a couple of times for a movie, shopping, or whatever, but I refuse to go to any parties and they have to go without me. When they talk about them later, I can tell that they're not telling me everything or everyone they saw, but I don't care. Well, I do, but I don't. I've got college applications, I've got studying, I've got exams, I've got plans. I've got my seventeenth birthday in less than two months—hallelujah!—but that means driving lessons with my dad.

Ugh.

"Let's try this again, Audrey. Bring your foot down on the clutch and put the car in reverse. When you have it in gear, ease up on the clutch. Okay. Back up slowly. That's it. Turn the wheel all the way to the left. To your left! LEFT!"

Mom had promised to take me but at the last minute changes her mind. I know what she's up to. Me and my dad haven't been getting along all that well or even speaking all that much since the infamous photo appeared in his e-mail box. She wants to bring us together. I think she could have picked a better way to do it, something that didn't involve the operation of large pieces of machinery and a whole lot of yelling.

"Don't do that! You'll burn out the clutch!"

"I'm sorry! I've been driving your car for exactly ninety seconds, okay?" I fiddle with the gearshift and try again.

"You've been riding around in this car for five years," he says. "You mean to tell me you never noticed how it sounded? You never paid attention to what I was doing? What did they teach you in Driver's Ed, anyway? I thought you were good with mechanical things."

The car bucks, stalls, and dies.

"Audrey!"

I don't bother to restart the car. "Dad, can't we take Mom's car out? That way I won't burn out your clutch and you won't give yourself an embolism screaming at me."

"Audrey, I'm not screaming."

"You're screaming."

"I've barely raised my voice. Anyway, you should know how to drive a standard. What if you're out with someone and they get sick?"

"Uh, I call an ambulance?"

"Not that sick, but sick enough that they can't drive and you have to?"

Oh, I get it. "You mean drunk, don't you? What if I'm out with some person who gets smashed and I have to drive him home?"

"Well, yes. It happens."

"I know, Dad."

He opens the glove compartment, takes out a napkin, and starts to dust the console. "I hope I don't have to remind you about the dangers of drinking and driving, Audrey."

"You don't."

"You can kill or injure yourself permanently. Or you could hurt someone else."

"Dad, I know that."

"If I catch you drinking and driving, I will personally bring you down to the jail myself."

"Thanks for the vote of confidence," I say.

"That's not what I meant," he says. "I'm just reminding you how dangerous drinking and driving is, that's all. It's not that I don't trust you."

Of course it is, but I nod anyway. That's my job. Nodding.

"I know that kids sometimes lose their heads, especially when they're seniors. Their parents go out of town, someone has a party, somebody gets the idea to steal from the liquor cabinet. Things can get out of control."

"In case you haven't noticed, I'm not going to any parties anymore," I say.

"Yes, well. Maybe there will be some that you'll want to go to later on. Spring parties. Or graduation parties."

More nodding.

"You have such a bright future ahead of you," he says.

Not if I drive this car into a telephone pole.

He stops wiping the dash and folds the paper towel into squares. "I don't want to see you hurt."

"Neither do I," I say.

"You'll be careful?" he says. "From now on?"

I don't need to ask what he means. "Yes, Dad. I'll be careful all the time."

Now *he* nods. "Good. Let's try this again."

January. We suffer through the last week of classes and then suffer more through finals, which means that classes change and I'm out of both history and study period—and Chilly is out of my face, hopefully forever. The thought of a totally Chilly-free semester is enough to keep me from crying over the short, dark days and the long, freezing nights. It's a gift that keeps on giving.

Ash has a gift of her own, a copy of the winter edition of *Ebb&Flow*, the literary magazine. (She's surrendered and named the edition "Tentacles.") It's a huge hit with the Goth and Emo kids. Pam and Cindy each get a copy and take turns reading the angriest poetry out loud to each other over lunch, alternating lines:

Pam: "*Beware, little boy, I am Death.*"

Cindy: "*The chemical cold in your gut.*"

Pam: "*The churn of rot in your head.*"

Cindy: "*I am the jerk in your knees.*"

Pam: "*And the ghost in your bed.*"

Cindy: "*I am the wet dream.*"

Pam: "*And the frozen dread.* Wait. Did you just say 'wet dream'?" She waves the pamphlet at Ash.

"They let you publish that?"

Ash shrugs. "We have advisors, but they're not much for advising. We pick what we want and wait for someone to notice. Any minute now, some mom will call and complain. But that's the fun part."

Pam flips through the pages. "Any more in here about wet dreams?"

"I don't think so."

"What about doing it?"

"Jesus!" says Ash.

"So," Joelle says to me. "What are we doing for your birthday?"

"I don't know."

"We have to do something! You're finally going to be seventeen."

"If I actually pass my road test, I'll drive you guys around in my dad's stick shift."

Pam says, "Oh, wow. The fun never stops with you, does it?"

"I know," says Joelle. "We'll all get dressed up and go to that new club. Stoke."

"A teen club?" says Pam. "They're so lame."

"We can't get into a real club. Come on," Joelle says. "It will be fun! I overheard Cherry Eames talking about it in the hallway." Joelle catch's Ash's expression. "What?"

"I'm not going to an under-twenty-one dance club.

And I'm not going anywhere Cherry Eames has been, okay?"

"Ash," Joelle says, "she doesn't own the place. I doubt she'll even go again, I—"

"I said I'm not going." Ash grabs her backpack and stomps out of the cafeteria.

Joelle's eyes tear up. "What did I say?"

I sigh. "You said the word 'Cherry.'"

"But that was so long ago!" Joelle says.

"Obviously not long enough," Pam says. "Not that I really know what the hell you guys are talking about."

"I'm going to go and make sure she's okay," I say, and run out of the cafeteria after Ash. She isn't in the hallway or by her locker, so I race out to the parking lot to see if her car's still there. It is. Even though it's like minus a hundred degrees, Ash is sitting in the backseat with the door wide open, sucking on a cigarette so hard that she'll need another one in about thirty seconds. I hug myself tightly and jog to her car.

"I don't want to talk," she says dully.

"Well, I want to get warm," I say. "How about we close the doors and turn up the heat?"

"Whatever," she says. She digs in her backpack and hands me the keys. I jump in the front seat and start the engine, cranking the heat all the way up. Then I get out of the car and push into the backseat with her, closing the door behind me. I crack the window so we don't asphyxiate ourselves. I shiver for a while until the heat comes on.

"So," I say, after my muscles stop twitching, "are you going to tell me what's going on?"

She rolls down her window, throws her butt out, and lights another cigarette. "Nobody took a picture of me, if that's what you're asking."

"Don't be a bitch," I say.

"I yam what I yam," she tells me, blowing smoke out the side of her mouth.

"Give me that," I say, grabbing for the butt.

She holds her arm away from me. "No!"

"Then tell me what's wrong."

"I told you. Nothing."

"Ash, you've been acting all weird for . . ."

"Stop," she says, looking hard at the ceiling. She swipes at her face. "Crap. I hate crying. It's so girly."

I wait.

"You remember Joelle's party?" She smacks herself in the head. "Well, duh, of course you remember that party. That's when Chilly took your picture."

"Yeah, let's forget about the picture, like, forever," I say. "What about the party?"

"While you were hanging out with Luke, Jimmy showed up."

"He did? Joelle never said anything!"

"I don't think she knows. Even if she saw him, she

probably wouldn't think anything of it. You know her. She thinks everything is 'such a long time ago.' She thinks yesterday is a long time ago."

This is totally true. "So Jimmy showed up. Was he with Cherry again?"

"No," she says. "He told me he broke up with her. He said he made a mistake when he cheated on me with her." Tears squeeze out of the corner of her eyes. "I believed him, and I . . ." She trails off.

"What?" I say.

"I . . ."

"Yeah?"

"I did him," she bursts out.

"You what?"

"On the floor of the bathroom. I am so dumb."

I'm confused. "But if he broke up with Cherry . . ."

"That lasted exactly one night," she says. "One. I went home and I was so . . . hopeful. Can you believe it? Me? Hopeful? But then I called him the next day and he . . ." More tears, mixed with her eyeliner, make tracks down her cheeks. "He tells me that they had a bad fight but that everything was okay. He went back to *her*, Aud. He went back to that twit." She shakes her head. "And then you tell me that you finally stopped messing around with Luke, and you were all proud of yourself, and I'd been on your case about it the whole time. *Don't lose your head, Audrey, watch what you're doing, Audrey,*" she says, mimicking herself.

I think about this. "That's why you got upset when I said that I did it with Luke?"

"Yeah. And here I am, the biggest idiot of all."

"Ash, why didn't you just tell me?"

"I couldn't." She shoots a plume of smoke into the air. "Why didn't you tell me that you'd done it with Luke?"

Oh, that. Well. "I felt stupid."

"Well, I *am* stupid."

"Stop it. You didn't know what Jimmy would do."

"He did it once before. Why did I think he wouldn't do it again?"

"Because you loved him?" I say.

She puts her face in her hands and sobs. I always thought Ash was so strong—that she could handle anything, stand up to anyone—that it's a shock to see her like this. So that she doesn't set her hair on fire, I take the cigarette from between her fingers and fling it outside. Then I put my arms around her and hug her. I tell her that Jimmy's the biggest loser clown boy ever known to women.

"More," she says, her voice muffled against my shoulder.

"More what?"

"Call him more names. I like the names. And creativity counts, just so you know."

"He's a flesh-eating lamprey. He's a penis-brained, pimple-headed pimp. He's a bottom-feeding, scum-sucking slut jockey."

She sniffs and pulls away from me. "Those are good. Even though I have no idea what a lamprey is."

"I'll submit them to the next edition of *Ebb&Flow*. I have connections there," I say.

"Okay," she says. "But I have to tell you that the chances of your stuff getting selected are slim. We get lots of pieces about scum-sucking slut jockeys." She tips her face up at me, streaky as Elvira's left out in the rain. "Are you mad at me?"

"For what?"

"For acting like such a jerk. I was so mean to you. I kept saying all those things about Luke, how he was such a player and all that."

"Oh, shut up. He *is* a player. You were worried about me."

"I *was* worried. But I think . . ." She plucks at the rip in her jeans. "I think I was jealous."

"Jealous? Jealous of what?"

"You seemed to like Luke so much. And he seemed to like you, too. As much as a guy like him can like anyone. Anyway, I wanted that feeling. And I knew I couldn't have it, and it seemed so unfair that anyone else had it, and it all ends up being for nothing anyway, because guys suck freaking rocks." Her face twists up. "I should have supported you. I should have been there for you. And I wasn't."

I'm about to argue, to say that she's always been there for me, but it's insane to deny that sometimes people fail each other. Maybe she wasn't there, not the way she could have been, but she's here now. And so am I.

"Listen," I say. "Here's what we're going to do."

"What?"

"We're going to sit here until spring."

Ash thinks a minute. "I'll run out of cigarettes."

"Who cares? Don't you know that smoking is so last decade?"

"What about food?"

"Nah. We need to lose a few pounds anyway."

"Speak for yourself," she says. She uses the hem of her T-shirt to wipe off her face. "You're starting to get roots. Time for another dye job."

"I'll dye it pink if you want. To match the tulips."

She exhales. "We stay till spring?"

"Till spring. I promise."

"Okay," she says. She leans back in the seat and so do I. We wriggle around to get more comfortable as the engine purrs us a sad winter song.

We don't stay in the car, of course. After about ten minutes, Ash is better, and more than that, bored, so we go back to the cafeteria. Then we have to spend the next ten minutes consoling Joelle, who is still upset for making Ash upset. Pam and Cindy get upset because they don't know the entire Jimmy/Ash/Cherry story, so we have to fill them in. Cindy tells us that it sounds a bit like *The Sweetest Vengeance,* a romance novel she's reading, and Ash informs her that bodice rippers are sexist fantasies that only feed into women's fears of owning their own sexuality. Cindy gets upset all over again. Pam has to buy all of us fries to shut us up.

It's a long lunch.

When I get home that afternoon, my mom's waiting in her usual spot in front of her laptop. But today she's not typing or drinking coffee, she's smiling big.

"What's up?" I say.

"We got some mail today." She waves a sheet of paper.

"Report cards? Gimme!"

I snatch the paper from her. Three A's. Four A pluses. A personal best. I sigh in relief. "I can't believe I got an A plus in Lambright's class."

"Audrey, look at the class rank."

"What? Why?" I've been number four forever. I scan the page. Class rank: 3/314. "I'm number *three?*"

"That's what the paper says."

"How's that possible?"

"Could be all those A pluses. You outdid yourself."
She pauses. "I hope that you can relax now. I hope this
makes you just a little bit happy."

I touch the number 3 on the page. "Almost," I say.
"Almost happy."

Spring, Sprang, Sprung

January turns into February. For my birthday I get a gift certificate from my friends, a silver necklace with a tiny cross from my parents, the continued cold shoulder from Luke, and a driver's license from the State of New Jersey. I borrow my mom's car so much that she complains she doesn't recognize it (or me) anymore.

In March, Ms. Godwin decides to go traditional for the spring musical: *Grease*. Joelle is trying to get Pam to try out for Rizzo. Pam is suspicious. She says she saw the movie once a long time ago but doesn't remember much besides a very young John Travolta in very tight pants.

"Who's Rizzo?"

"She's mean, she's sarcastic, she's smooth. She's the leader of the Pink Ladies."

"I don't remember any Pink Ladies. Are they lesbians?"

"No!" says Joelle. "They're like a girl gang. Except that they don't beat anyone up or kill anyone."

"Well, what do they do?"

"They just go around acting cool."

"Sounds boring," says Pam.

"It's so not boring. It's fun! You'd be perfect, I swear. I'll help you learn the part."

Pam shakes her head. "This is really not my thing, you know."

"I'm telling you, you'll love it. You get to dress up in these great fifties costumes and sing these songs . . ."

"Sing! I'm not singing anything!"

Joelle puts her hands on her hips. "Pam, you never study and you don't do any of your homework. You don't have a job. You hang around the theater at every rehearsal. Plus, you've given up on guys, right? What else do you have to do?"

Cindy nods. "She has a point."

Pam crooks a finger at Cindy. "I'll try out if she tries out."

"But I don't want to try out!" Cindy says.

"And I'm not the only one who's going to make a fool of myself," Pam says. "So you're trying out, too."

They both do. Pam doesn't sing well or act well, and she forgets a few lines, but she has a kind of presence that makes you want to watch her, some sort of razor-y, grit-your-teeth, man-eater thing. You see why people fall for it. Ms. Godwin does, anyway. Pam gets the part. Joelle snares the lead, Sandy, and her brand-new boyfriend, O/Joe, will play the male lead, Danny Zuko. Cindy ends up on the crew with me, which suits her just fine. Ash promises to attend the rehearsals and write terrible tentacle poetry about the set and the performances.

"Ooh! Black bile!" I say.

"Frozen dread!" says Pam.

A new play means another Slut City World Tour road trip to the Home Depot, and also to the junkyard, where I can buy an old car door and some panels for the "Greased Lightning" sequence. And it also means more hammering and sanding and painting, more pizza for the minions, more hours spent at the theater listening to Ms. Godwin bark at Pam for trying to read her lines off her cell phone and at Joelle for not learning them fast enough.

Nobody's fast enough. Mid-April, two weeks before the show opens, Ms. Godwin wants to know when the sets will be finished.

"We don't have that much more to do," I tell her. "Some painting and some assembly. It shouldn't take long."

She's wearing some sort of capelike scarf that's fastened at the throat with a large jeweled brooch. She tugs at the brooch and looks down her nose at me. "I'm surprised at you, Audrey. I've never seen you as behind as you've been this past month or so."

I think we're right on schedule, but that's not the kind of thing you say to Ms. Godwin. You say, "I'm sorry, Ms. Godwin. I'm working as fast as I can."

"Hmmm. . .," she says. "Well. I suppose you've been distracted."

"Excuse me?"

She heaves one of her why-must-I-spell-everything-out sighs. "I don't like to get involved in the personal affairs of my students, but I have to say that I thought you of all people would have had better judgment."

I feel a cold flame in my cheeks, as if someone has pressed ice cubes to my skin. "What do you mean?"

"Audrey, I do have eyes and ears, even if I don't always comment on everything I see and hear. I thought you were far too smart to put yourself in that position." She realizes what she's said, and I see *her* cheeks flush.

"But I am glad it wasn't worse for you."

This is the woman who wanted us to turn *Hamlet* upside down. What about a little female solidarity? A little support? I'm so mad I want to pound a nail into her head. "You know what, Ms. Godwin?" I say, the words practically shredding my vocal cords. "I have to say that *I* think it's been bad enough for me. And you know what else? I would have thought that you of all people would be a little more understanding."

I stomp out of the auditorium and over to my locker. It's close to seven o'clock, and I'm tired, sweaty, totally pissed off, and covered with dust and paint. I'm standing in front of my open locker, yanking on my jacket, checking my pockets for my precious car keys—okay, my mom's precious car keys—and thinking that if Ms. Godwin threw me off the design team it would be okey-dokey with me, when the door at the other end of the hallway opens. I'm not alone anymore. Luke's in the hall with me. He's wearing his baseball uniform, his mitt tucked underneath his arm. He's as dirty and sweaty as I am—dirtier, sweatier.

I freeze, he freezes.

We stare at each other. His eyes flick to my head, where I've knotted my hair—now even darker than before—in a crazy, fraying ball, and I just now remember that I have pencils sticking through it. I look him up and down, take in the smudges on his forehead and cheeks, take in those stupid short pants they make the baseball players wear. It annoys me that Luke can make kneesocks look good.

I don't know what to say. Hi? I love you? I hate you? You make my guts twist? Where'd you get those rockin' socks?

I say: "Love the knickers."

His head jerks back as if I'd slapped him. I can see him debating whether he wants to talk to me or not, but then he says, "What *is* your problem?"

I jam my arm into my jacket. "I don't have any problems. Not anymore."

He walks toward me. "What's that supposed to mean?"

"Exactly what I said."

He stops about five feet away. The shine in his eye says that he'd like to slap me for real. "Let's get one thing straight: I didn't take that picture. You know I couldn't have taken it. None of my friends took it. I didn't pay anyone to do it or talk anyone into doing it. And I didn't send it to anyone. I know you know this, I heard what happened with Chilly. This. Was. Not. Me. None of it was my fault."

"I didn't say it was."

"Then what is up with you?"

"I don't know what you're talking about," I say. I slam my locker shut and spin the lock.

"You look at me as if I just poisoned your cat. Your *friends* look at me as if I just poisoned your cat. I'm freaking sick of it. What did I ever do to you?"

His face is red, and the veins in his neck stand out. I've never seen him mad before. It feels good to be able to make him mad. And then it feels weird. Why should I care if he's mad or not? Why should I care at all?

"Nobody's looking at you like anything," I say. "Get over yourself."

He shakes his head. "Never mind. You're crazy." He spins around to go back where he came from, the magical land of untouchable boys who flit around on their magical golden wings, wearing their magical kneesocks.

But he changes his mind and turns to me again. "They all know it was me in the picture. Everyone knows. They knew as soon as they saw it."

"You think that makes a difference?" I say. "Were you dropped on your head as a baby? Nobody cares whether it was you. Nobody cares what you did. Actually, it just makes you more popular." I zip up my jacket. "It makes me a slut."

"Come on," he says. "You're not a slut."

"Great," I say, "I'll go home and inform my dad. He's been a little confused since someone e-mailed him some porn starring his only daughter."

He has the grace to wince at the dad bit, I'll give him

that. "I'm sorry," he says. "But I didn't have anything to do with it."

I was tired before, and I'm getting more tired. "Whatever," I say. "It doesn't matter. Most people have forgotten about it anyway."

"Except you," he says.

Except me, except Ms. Godwin, except everyone. I can't imagine a day I'll ever be free of this stupid picture. And I've had enough of the whole thing. I don't want to talk about it ever again, especially not with him. I pick up my backpack and swing it up on my shoulder. "I gotta go. I'm sure you've got places to be, games to play, girls to do."

"God! What is wrong with you? You dumped me, remember?"

I almost drop my backpack. "Dumped you? I didn't dump you."

He doesn't look mad, he looks furious. "Really? What was ''Bye, have a nice life' supposed to mean, then?"

"But. . ." I say. I'm totally baffled. I *had* dumped him, but I didn't know *he* would see it that way. You had to be going out for someone to dump you. Did he actually think. . . ???

"How could I dump you when we weren't even going out?" I say.

"We were doing something," he mumbles, almost under his breath.

I can't believe what I'm hearing; that's exactly what I said to Ash. "What?"

"Forget it," he says. "I'm out of here." He stalks away, his cleats clicking on the tiles.

"Wait," I say, running after him. I grab his arm. "If that's what you thought, that we were . . . doing something, why didn't you say anything? Why were you with all those other girls?" I can't help it, my eyes start to tear up. I can finally understand how Ash has been so pissed for so long.

He yanks his arm away from me. "What other girls?"

"All the other girls," I say. "I mean, every party we were at, you made sure you flirted with every stupid girl in the room."

"I'm friends with them."

"Right," I say.

"So I like to talk to people. So I like to talk to girls. That doesn't mean I did anything with them, at least not after I knew."

"Not after you knew what?"

His breaths come short and hard, and he looks at the row of lockers as he answers. "Not after I knew that you might be into me. The pool party, when you followed me to my car. After that day, I always ended up with you." He doesn't seem happy about telling me this.

I shake my head. "You never talked to me at school. You barely even said 'hey' to me in the hallways. It was like I didn't exist."

"I didn't talk to you because you didn't talk to me! I'd say two words and you looked like you were going to puke. You couldn't sprint away fast enough. And at all those parties, I thought you were avoiding me. I thought you didn't want anything serious. What was I supposed to do, follow you around like that freak Chillman? Is that what you wanted?"

No, I couldn't have been so wrong. It's not possible. I take a deep breath. "So what about Pam Markovitz?"

"What about her?"

"Why'd you screw her?"

"*What?*"

"You heard me."

"Now I know you're crazy. I didn't do Pam Markovitz."

"Liar," I say.

"Who told you that? Pam? Who knows how many guys she's—"

"Shut up about Pam," I say. "You don't know her. And Pam wasn't the one who told me."

"Then who did?"

I don't say anything. I'm not seeing Luke and the empty hallway, I'm seeing Jessica Berger's basement the way it was six months ago, two weeks before Halloween. I'm seeing Ash talking to Nardo, looking like she'd gnaw off her own arm to get away from him.

I see Cindy Terlizzi and Joelle and Ray Dale and all the usuals, but I don't see Luke, and I don't see Pam Markovitz. I start to panic. He's talking to her, he's with her, she knows what to do, she's not afraid, she likes it, she's better than me, she's done it lots of times before. And then I hear Chilly whispering in my ear: *Looking for your boyfriend? He's a little busy right now. Guess who he's with? You'll never, ever guess, or maybe you will. Just wait, any minute now, they'll come down together.* And then they do. Pam Markovitz first, and Luke right after her. She flips her hair and says something to him and he smiles, his teeth flashing. I see myself putting my drink on the table and walking right out of the house and all the way home.

Luke's dropped his mitt to the floor and he's gripping my shoulders. "Hey," he says, "who told you that I was with Pam? Who?" He shakes me just a little and my shoulders curl in toward my heart.

I look down at the tile, where his cleats have left clots of reddish dirt. "Chilly."

He lets go of me. "Chillman told you."

I nod.

"The guy who took that picture of us and sent it around to every cell phone in the country."

I nod again.

"And you believed him?"

I feel the imprint of his hands on my arms. If I have

to nod once more, I think my neck will break.

Luke reaches down, scoops up his glove, slips his left hand inside it. "So you bought what your psycho ex-boyfriend told you without even asking me if it was true." He punches his glove with his fist. "Now who's the one who's been dropped on her head?" He pushes past me and leaves me standing there alone.

Sinner, Repent

It's one of those fiercely sunny late-April days that make you think it's warmer than it really is. I huddle in the pew in the short-sleeve shirt I thought would be perfect today but totally isn't and watch the light shoot through the stained-glass windows. Blazing and bright, the church looks like God herself decided to drop in and decorate the place, like she's letting me know that maybe, just maybe, she might forgive me for being the biggest, most horrible, gullible self-involved moron that ever lived.

I think it's kind of nice that she'd send the sun as a signal, nice that she'd consider forgiving me.

Also handy, because I don't plan on forgiving myself anytime soon.

My mother pats my hand. "We're so proud of you," she says. For a minute, I don't know what she's talking about. And then I remember. The acceptance letters. I've gotten two, one from Columbia and one from Cooper Union—my two top choices. Just like that, I know where I'm going to be for the next four years. Studying architecture in New York City. All I have to do is choose one school or the other.

I should be happier.

Pastor Narcolepsy steps up to the pulpit. Something's different about him—he's all spry, even twitchy. At first I think that he's finally discovered the virtues of coffee. But it turns out that he's been doing some thinking. About sex. And, for the first time in forever, he's actually awake.

"I was watching a television program the other day, a program interrupted by a commercial for a video. The only point of this video, it seemed, was to show young women exposing themselves at parties and on vacation in exotic places. The girls were all smiling and looked like they were having a wonderful time. And of course, the young men in the video seemed to be having even more fun than the girls were.

"It occurred to me that this is happening all too often in our culture today. Young women seem to subscribe to the 'less is more' theory of fashion, which these videos take to the extreme, and young men seem to be in no hurry to denounce the trend. Not that the latter is surprising."

We laugh, not because the joke is so funny but because we're all in shock. Pastor N.? Awake? And talking about topless girls on spring break in Cancun? What the heck is going on? My dad is sitting so still that he could be a cat. My mom sneaks glances at me.

"My point is that young women are being increasingly objectified in movies, TV, games, and music videos. We are so used to seeing these images that I don't think we really register them anymore. But in our culture, women are becoming less than *people* worthy of respect and more simply *objects* to be admired, or even used and abused. They are things. And things, as we all know, are disposable. What these girls don't understand, and what young men don't seem to understand, is that this is demeaning to both the user and the used."

Pastor Narcolepsy scans the audience as if he can tell who's been used and who's been doing some using just by looking at us. I feel like he's looking right at me, and I slip down lower in the pew. I'm colder than I was before; the skin on my arms is rough and yellowish, like a plucked chicken's.

"Would it surprise you to hear that human sexuality is a holy thing, a gift given to us by God? In Genesis, we learn that Adam and Eve came together 'naked and unashamed' because they experienced sex as a spiritual as well as a physical communion. A meeting of soul mates. In contrast to this deeply spiritual and a physical communion, this profoundly joyous experience, sex that is a product of mere lust can't even begin to reach the same heights. This is why Jesus condemned it. He thought that lust made sex less than it ought to be—sacramental. Holy."

Great, my lust has condemned me. My lust has made me cheap. Bring me a scarlet letter and I'll wear it on my forehead. "S" for slut. "S" for stupid. "S" for sin, for smash, for splinter.

"Why do we often feel so lost and guilty when we've had lustful thoughts or had meaningless sexual encounters?" says the pastor.

I don't know, maybe when you assume someone thought you were just a piece of ass and then you turned around and treated *him* like one?

"It's because we have desensitized ourselves, we have reduced sex to a cheap hormonal response. We have forgotten the holiness of this sacred act. Sex was not given to us to *create* intimacy; sex was given to us so that we can *express* intimacy, the intimacy that already exists with our spouses. It is the ultimate fulfillment of the marriage vow."

Interesting message. Teenagers, sex is AMAZING. And you can't have any.

Pastor Narcolepsy is on such a roll that he gets chummy with the congregation. "Listen, guys, sex is so important and so vital a gift that it is simply not an act to take cheaply or lightly."

I can feel my dad tense up next to me; I can feel how much he wants to grab me and start screaming, *ARE YOU LISTENING TO THIS? ARE YOU HEARING THIS?* I wonder if he slipped the pastor a request and a few dollars, like you do when you want the DJ to play that special song. I suppose this is a do-as-I-say-and-not-as-I-do situation.

My mom reaches out and pats my leg. Pat, pat, pat. "P" for pat!

"I work with a youth ministry, and some of the kids I counsel can tell you stories that would make your hair curl! One boy, a thoughtful, delightful teenager, has recently renounced his sexual past and now tries to live life anew. 'Pastor,' he tells me, 'I'm a born-again virgin.' Of course no one can turn back the clock and regain one's virginity, but one can turn away from one's mistakes and let God help us forge a new path."

Pastor's got lots more to say about sex and about Jesus and about God and about those crazy "young people" who don't understand how they're cheapening themselves and each other. He goes on and on and on. I start to tune out. I get it, I get it—he might as well be cracking me on the head with a frying pan—but I'm all confused anyway. Maybe—because I am the most repulsive, disgusting, loathsome sinner, one of those crazy, lustful young people destined to appear in a "Girls Gone Wild" video—maybe God will suck back her bright and cheerful spring light and never ever ever forgive me, but all that talk about touching bodies and touching souls makes me think about Luke, about the one and only time we actually did it (the one time we had cheap and meaningless physical—and totally unspiritual—intercourse as the result of mere hormonal responses).

But that's the problem—it didn't feel that way. Not cheap. Not meaningless.

Which is probably why the whole thing got me into so much trouble.

Love Hammer

$\mathcal{E}$arly October, late on a Saturday night. I got a message.

    Instant Message with **"salvs42"**
    Last message received at: 11:32:07 PM
    salvs42: doin anything tomorrow?
    audball113: not much
    salvs42: having peple over wanna come?
    audball113: K what time
    salvs42: 2
    audball113: sounds good

I sat at my computer for a long time. Luke had never IM'd me before. I'd never seen his house before. Was it just another party? Did it mean anything? Ash would say no. Ash would say that he was just trying to get some.

Ash was right. And she was wrong, too. Because Luke wasn't the only one.

Sunday, I told my mom I was going to Ash's, Ash that I was going to Joelle's, Joelle that I was studying, and walked the ten blocks to Luke's house. I was the only "people" to show up. Luke and a very small, very excited cotton ball met me at the door. The cotton ball danced all around my shoes, sniffing and yipping as Luke let me inside.

"Down, Daisy," Luke said.

"She's so cute," I said. "Hey, Daisy." I bent down to pet her and she spun around and around in a teeny doggy frenzy. She licked my hand as if it were a slab of liver.

I smiled up at Luke. "I would have figured you more as the German shepherd type."

"Nah," he said. "Daisy attracts all the chicks." Luke scooped up the dog. "Let's go to the den."

"Where is everyone else?"

"They'll show up later, maybe."

"Oh," I said, butterflies boinging off my stomach walls. For now, we had the house to ourselves.

We walked down a hallway, past the kitchen and into the family room. Pictures of Luke and his brothers crowded every wall and table. I wanted to inspect them all, but I was afraid I'd seem too nosy. I did pick up a picture of an older couple in identical pleated pants. Both were blond, but the man had a neatly trimmed beard. Still, they looked almost exactly alike.

"These are your parents?" I asked.

Luke peered over my shoulder. "Yep, that's the twins."

"They do look like twins," I said. "Except for the beard."

"We keep trying to get Mom to grow one," he said, "but she won't go for it."

"Where are they?"

"Visiting my aunt on Long Island. They won't be back till tonight." He put Daisy on the floor. "Do you want something to drink?"

"Sure," I said. "Whatever you have."

I sat down while he disappeared into the kitchen with Daisy on his heels. I inhaled, trying to identify the scent of the house. Everyone's house smells different, some in good ways and some in not-so-good ways—like burned cabbage or cat pee or whatever. Luke's house smelled like lemon furniture polish with a hint of boy. It smelled happy.

Luke came back with two Cokes and a couple of

straws. "If you want a glass, I can get you one."

"This is good," I said.

He sat down next to me. Daisy jumped on the coffee table and stared at me as if I were supposed to be supplying the entertainment. I peeked at Luke and thought about the entertainment, what I could do to supply it. I felt all shaky inside, my ligaments twanging, my temples pounding. Would it be strange if I put my Coke on the table and jumped him? Probably. I should sit here for at least five more minutes before I did anything like that, right? Maybe ten minutes. So what were we going to do for ten whole minutes? There was usually a party going on all around us, I usually had to wait for at least an hour to get his attention. This was too weird.

"I like that picture," I said, pointing at a large photo on the wall. It was a black-and-white portrait of Daisy, but the focus and perspective were odd—her face sharp and clear, but the rest of her small and fading out. Kind of cool and kind of funny at the same time.

"Thanks," he said. "I took that."

"You did?"

"Yup. I've got some more in an album in my room. Do you want to see them?"

It was a line, maybe, but what did I care? I was having an out-of-body experience again, or, more accurately, an in-the-body experience. Why else was I there? "Okay," I said.

I followed him out of the den, down the hallway, up the stairs, and into his room, Daisy running ahead of us, claws clicking. I was surprised that the room wasn't the usual blue—it was orange, with a wood floor and a rumpled bed with red sheets, blankets, and pillows. It had your typical guy stuff: bookcases with loose stacks of books and pictures, a pile of sneakers, a desk with a computer, and some pages from the *Sports Illustrated* swimsuit edition tacked on the wall, along with your usual row of sports trophies of different sizes, some team photographs, and a signed baseball. Not neat, not messy, the room was sort of pleasantly disorganized, like a set designer had carefully arranged everything for maximum effect before the play was about to start. The boy smell was stronger in here, too: musky, the way the crook of Luke's neck smelled when I pressed my nose there. My toes curled up in my shoes.

"Sorry about the mess," he said. He pulled some clothes off a chair threw them on the floor. Then he opened a drawer in his desk, fished out a photo album, and handed it to me. I sat down and paged through the album, expecting to see more doggy photos, but found mostly black-and-white portraits. Some of his family, some of other random people, a lot of them girls. (I wondered if he kept some extra girls in the closet or in the basement for when he was bored.)

But the photos were good, some of them really good.

I stared at a hot girl I didn't know with this cutie-pie spray of freckles across her nose. I immediately hated her, but loved the picture. "These are great," I said.

He sat down on the bed, Daisy on his lap. "Thanks. My dad just bought me a new camera. Well, it's an old camera from the fifties. Called a Hasselblad. Maybe I can take one of you sometime?"

"Maybe," I said. It occurred to me that I had no idea what his plans for the future were—or if he even had any kinds of plans, if he wanted to stay in high school forever. "Are you going to study photography somewhere?"

He shrugged. "I don't know. Most of the schools I applied to have some sort of photography classes, just in case I want to take some. But I'm not sure what I want to do yet."

I didn't know what to say to that. A lot of people didn't seem to know what they wanted to do, but I couldn't understand it at all. How can you not have any plans? "Where'd you apply?"

"Mostly around here. Rutgers, Penn, a few other places."

"What's the top choice?"

He grinned. "Wherever I get in. And then whoever comes up with the most money, I guess. I'm hoping for some sports scholarships."

"Oh," I said.

"So where are you going to go? Princeton? Harvard? Yale?"

"All of them," I said. "I'm triple-majoring." I didn't say anything more in case I lost my nerve and began babbling uncontrollably about architecture and interior design and a thousand other massively unsexy things he probably couldn't care less about.

"Well," he said. "That's good." He lifted Daisy and then set her down on the floor. "You know, you're kind of far away over there."

I felt a little jolt. "I am, aren't I?"

"How about coming over here?" he said.

I put the album on the desk, stood up, and went over to the bed. All the other times that we'd found some corner or some car to make out in, I never knew exactly what was going to happen, exactly what I might do. But standing in front of the bed, his bed, with his happy boy scent filling my nose, I knew. I had a condom in the pocket of my jeans, one from a package that I'd snuck out and bought myself even though I'd had to wear sunglasses and the cashier guy gave me his best girls-don't-buy-condoms-don't-do-it-you're-too-young-and-where-the-hell's-your-mother frown. A small part of my brain, the good girl part, squeaked, *Are you sure? Are you absolutely sure?* I told it to shut up and go take a nap.

I didn't wait for Luke to make a move, I didn't even wait to climb up onto the bed. I stood in front of him, grabbed his face in my hands, and kissed him, slipping my tongue between his teeth, resisting the urge to swallow his face right there. He growled and pulled me onto the mattress. As we kissed, I felt this ache building, an ache that started between my legs but radiated outward like it was traveling along my veins, tightening and expanding and tightening again. He yanked the covers over us and yanked at my clothes—sweater, T-shirt, bra, jeans. He slid his hand inside my underwear and I wasn't sure which one of us gasped. I felt his lips moving against my ear. "Is it okay if I. . . ?"

"Yeah," I said against his throat. And then the underwear was gone, too, tossed off the side of the bed. He stripped down so fast it was as if his clothes were made of Velcro. Rubbing against his bare skin was so yummy that I had to keep myself from humming.

I came up for air. "Are you sure your parents won't be home for a while?"

"They'll be gone for hours," he said.

"And what about your friends?"

"What friends?"

"The ones you invited over?"

"Oh, them. I think they've been delayed indefinitely."

"Good," I said. Now that I was here, now that we were doing it or about to, I wanted to see him, I wanted to see everything. I thought about asking him to stand up and pose, I thought about throwing the covers back so that I could get a better look, but then I thought about how the sunlight might give *him* a better look, and I wasn't up for that. So I reached down and let my fingers see everything for me, imprint it all in my head. The half-moons of his hips. The muscles of his thighs. The crisp, springy hair, so different from the shiny waves on the top of his head. I brushed past his hard-on and cupped the delicate sac underneath as gently as I could, the way you would a baby bird, amazed that a person could have something this fragile on the outside of his body, unhidden, unprotected. It was like having a gall-bladder or a lung pasted on your skin. I rolled those small glands in my fingers until he moaned and put his hand on top of mine.

"Audrey . . ."

I interrupted him. "I brought something with me."

He got quiet. Then: "You did?"

"Yes."

"I have something, too. Where's yours?"

"In my pocket."

He turned and reached over the side of the bed, scratching around for my jeans. The curve of his back was the most incredible thing I'd ever seen. I had the strangest urge to bite him, which kind of freaked me out.

He turned to me with the blue square in his hand. "Is this your first time?"

"It's okay," I said.

"You might bleed."

I didn't ask how he knew this. "I'm fine," I said. He didn't seem *that* big. How much could I possibly bleed?

"I don't want to hurt you."

And people said girls talked a lot; he was ruining the mood with all the Mr. Sensitive blah-blah-blah. I didn't want to *talk*. I didn't want to *think*. I'd done enough of that to last through my next four lives. I'd been responsible. I'd gone and bought the condom. What else was there?

"You can stop with the chitchat now."

I got a small smile for that one. "Yes, ma'am."

With his teeth, he ripped open the package, and his hands disappeared under the blankets. Then he rolled on top of me, an elbow on either side of my face. He kissed me as he pressed against me, poking me with his spongy self, now rubber-coated. I thought about the spam I always got in my e-mail box—"BE A LOVE HAMMER ALL NIGHT LONG!" I wasn't sure if he and his love hammer would ever find their way inside, so I put my hand down to help him. I felt a surge and a sharp, stinging pain.

"Are you all right?" he said.

"Yeah," I told him, though I wasn't sure. I didn't know what I expected—well, okay, I expected something a lot less weird, a lot better. Even though I'd heard a girl's first time pretty much sucks, who wants to believe it? This felt too bizarre, stranger when he started moving. It was like an alien had jammed itself up into my body, an alien with rough skin that stretched and scratched me. If this was sex, I thought, it wasn't very good at all.

But I put my arms around him and hugged him, because I didn't know what else to do. He kept kissing me, bending my leg and curling one arm under my knee, and sliding his other arm around my shoulders. I didn't understand what he was doing, but I let him do it. Maybe he saw it in a movie and thought it would be fun, or maybe this was how everyone did it—what did I know? I tried to focus on the kissing part, though he was sort of spacing out on that end. His movements changed from pushing to a kind of rocking. As he rocked me, I felt the stretchiness and scratchiness fade away to a sort of friction. *Oh,* I thought. *This isn't bad.* Not great, not seeing stars and rainbows and fireworks, but okay.

And then I saw Luke's face. His eyes were screwed shut and his mouth hung open. I watched him, though I could hardly stand to see someone like that, all naked like that. It seemed rude to stare, but I couldn't help it. And the little muffled gasps were worse: listening to them was like hearing someone crying through a locked bathroom door. I hugged tighter because he seemed to need it.

He moaned again, and the rocking went back to

pushing. His face twisting as if I were strangling him, he shuddered before collapsing on top of me. I thought the shuddering would stop, but it didn't—he shivered like he was freezing. "Are *you* all right?" I asked him.

"Yeah," he said, and kept shivering.

I thought it would be okay if I stroked his hair, so that's what I did. I massaged his neck and patted his back as he shook. I don't know how long I did that. It was a while. He was so heavy, so heavy he could fall through the bed, but I knew he wouldn't because I was holding him up.

What they don't show you in movies: the aftermath. People trying to remove their parts from other people's parts without losing their grip on a squashygushy condom; locating the box of tissues they believe is way under the bed without actually getting *out* of the bed; dressing underneath the blankets—one of you, anyway—then having to remove the clothes and put them on again because they were backwards or inside out; family pets jumping all over the comforter because they think you're playing a really cool game of doggy-catch-my-toes; people not quite looking each other in the eye because that could get too, you know, personal.

When we finally got up, I saw the sheets and slapped a hand over my mouth. I thought, *Is that from ME, or was a lamb sacrificed here?* I didn't know what to say; even on the red sheets you could tell. "I'm sorry, I'm so sorry," I said. "I didn't think it would happen like that."

"Don't worry about it. I'll wash them," he said.

"Cold water," I told him. "You have to use cold water or the blood won't come out."

"Okay," he said.

"Now," I told him. I started hauling the sheets off the bed.

"I can do it later," he said.

"It'll leave a stain," I said, so embarrassed that I felt like I was losing height as I spoke. "If your mom ever makes your bed for you . . ." I trail off.

He considered this. "Good point."

We gathered up the sheets and the mattress pad and dragged them downstairs to the laundry room in the basement. Luke watched as I used detergent to scrub out most of the blood and then dumped about a half a bottle more soap in with the sheets. I flipped the machine on, sighing in relief as I closed the lid. No stains. At least not ones that would show up very well.

We went back upstairs. In addition to the humiliation over the carnage I'd left, I felt all raw and open—the word "open" meant all sorts of things it never had before—and I wanted a bath. Also, I wanted to be by myself and chill. I never believed that virginity was some sort of precious gift or whatever, and I never believed it was something I'd "save" till marriage, but I did feel as if I'd given something away. I hoped that it was something that you could give over and over again, hoped that eventually you got something in return, but I didn't know what that could be and didn't know when I'd know.

I told Luke that I had to go, that I had a test to study for—which was true, which was always true. He didn't argue. He and Daisy walked me to the door. "Thanks for coming over," he said.

I nodded. "Thanks for asking."

He shuffled his feet. "So I guess I'll see you," he said.

I almost laughed, it was so lame. After all that wanting? All that blood? How did it become so lame? "I guess."

But then he reached out and brushed the hair from my cheek. "Don't study too hard," he said.

"I will."

He kept his hand where it was, his thumb touching my lips. I heard the words before he said them: "I know you will."

Born Again

After church, while waiting for Joelle,

Cindy, and Pam, I tell Ash about arguing with

Luke in the hallway after school, about how mad

he was, how stupid and horrible I was. Angel is

officially closed for inventory today, but we sit

whispering on the floor in the prom dress section

of the store, far away from the back office, where

my dad is ripping through a pile of paperwork.

"Jesus," says Ash, "Luke actually, like, *liked* you all along?"

"I think so," I tell her. "Maybe."

"Whoa," she says. "And you were such a bitch to him. Worse, you were like this crazy stalker *psycho-bitch*."

"I thought he was with other people. I thought he slept with Pam. And for a while I wondered if he had something to do with the picture," I say.

Ash shakes her head. "You're so weird." She counts off on her fingers. "First you're doing this casual thing, then you're with him every weekend, then you do it with him, then you're not casual anymore, then you think he's slept with someone else because Chilly—hello? ew?—said he did, then you blow him and break up with him in the same night, then someone takes a picture of you, and then you decide to be friends with the girl you think Luke slept with. Does any of this make sense to you?"

I wince. "Feel free to shut up at any time."

"I'm just trying to understand."

"I didn't want to be one of those girls who doesn't get mad at the guy when he cheats, who only gets mad at the girls he cheats *with*, okay? Besides, I thought he was playing everyone. It wasn't about Pam. It was about him."

"And now it's about you. What are you going to do?"

"Nothing," I say, miserable. "What can I do? I screwed everything up. So not only am I a slut, I'm a slut who isn't having any kind of sex. What is up with that?"

Ash winds Angel's single available boa around her neck. "All I can say is that I'm glad I'm me and not you."

"Thanks," I say.

"You never did tell me about it, you know," she says, spitting a feather out of her mouth.

"Tell you about what?"

"Doing it," she says. "How was it?"

"Well. . . ," I begin. When I get to the part about the bloody sheets, Ash pulls a Joelle and falls to the floor.

"Ack! Gross!" she says. "I can't believe you had to do his laundry."

"I couldn't leave it like that," I say. "Could you?"

"We read *Forever*. You should have used a towel."

"*Forever* didn't say anything about losing four quarts of blood."

Ash pats my hand. "Next time you won't need the towel."

"Next time?" I say. "There isn't going to be a next time."

"No next time for what?" Joelle says, running over and flopping down to the floor next to me. She's got the goofiest smile on her face, a smile she's had since she started dating O/Joe.

Ash wags the boa at her. "Audrey doesn't think she'll ever have sex again."

Pam and Cindy push through the racks of purple and pink dresses. "Join the club," says Pam.

"What do you mean? Why won't you have sex again?" Joelle shrieks.

"Shhh!" I say. "My dad's in the back."

"Go ahead," says Ash. "Tell them the story."

They all sit on the floor so that I can go over the whole thing. Pam nods sympathetically, but Cindy covers her mouth with both hands and Joelle looks a little pale.

"I read somewhere that you won't bleed if you did lots of gymnastics or rode horses when you were little. I did both of those," says Joelle. "You don't think I'll bleed like that, do you?" I figure she must have big plans for O/Joe to be asking that question.

"Everybody bleeds," says Pam, sounding a bit like an extra from an action movie. "No big deal. Doesn't even hurt that much."

"Were you upset?" says Joelle. "Were you so so so embarrassed?"

"Yes, Joelle. I was. And please keep saying it exactly like that, because it makes me feel so so so much better."

Cindy pipes up. "In some cultures the fathers take the bloody sheets and parade around the town with them after their daughters' wedding nights to prove their daughters were virgins."

"Did you read that in one of your books?" Ash says sarcastically.

"I saw it on the History Channel, for your information!"

"Great," I say. "And I didn't even save the sheets. I'm going to bring shame on my family."

"I guess we'll have to stone you," Ash says.

"I don't want to stone anyone before we pick out our prom gowns," Joelle says.

"*Our* gowns?" says Ash. "I'm not going to the prom. I'm here to help you."

"But I thought that guy, what's-his-name, asked you to go," Joelle says.

"Who? Nardo? I'm not going with Nardo," Ash says.

"Why not?" I ask her. "What's wrong with Nardo?"

"Nothing," she says. "I don't want to go with him, that's all." Her face has her don't-ask-me-any-questions-or-I'll-light-a-cigarette-and-burn-you-a-new-eye-socket expression, so I leave it alone.

"What about you, Pam?" Joelle says. "Aren't you going?"

"No way," says Pam. "I've given up on stupid high school stuff, and proms have to be the stupidest high school stuff there is."

"Nobody asked me," says Cindy. "I want to go, but . . . ." She trails off, plucking wistfully at a fluffy pink number that would make anyone look like a giant cupcake.

"I'm not going, either," I say.

"No!" says Joelle. "I cannot be the only one of us going to the prom! That's not right!"

"But that's the way it is," says Pam. "So why don't we just pick out your dress and get the hell out of here. All this pink and purple crap is making me nervous."

"I don't want to go if you guys aren't there," Joelle wails. "I mean, I'll go anyway, but . . ."

"I might go if I could wear one of those," Pam says, waving her hand toward the wedding gowns. "That would be funny."

I laugh. "It would be, wouldn't it?" I think about what Pastor Narcolepsy said, about people trying to let go of their past mistakes. But I don't think he understood what the real mistakes were. Even though he talked about a guy calling himself a born-again virgin, we all knew that it was the girls he was talking to. I know I was supposed to fight Luke off. That's what girls do, isn't it? You can only do this much and go this far, and then only if he promises to love you forever. Or you can do anything and everything, but only because the guys want it and it's what you have to do to keep them around; it's not really your fault—you know guys, they're just big walking erections, ha ha. No one ever talks about what girls want, because we're not *supposed* to want anything, not really. No one talks about how hard you have to fight yourself sometimes. No one tells you about how the want gets in your blood, eating everything in its path, how every time you hear a certain name, or see a certain face, the cells divide and multiply and you are just. so. hungry.

How do brides wear white when we're all sinners? I have a friend who likes to call himself a born-again virgin. . . .

I'll give them born-again virgins.

"Hey," I say, "I have an idea."

Because Joelle's the only one who has a date, it takes us a while to convince her to go along.

"Come on, Joelle," I say. "It will be so great, all five of us together. So much better than going with a guy. No arguments, no bad breakups on the dance floor, no mistakes. Just us, the Born-Again Virgins, wiping out the past."

"What are you talking about? What past?" Joelle says.

"It's ironic," I say. "We're not really wiping out the past. We can't. Nobody can. We're just making a statement."

"But I'm not a born-again virgin! I'm an *actual* virgin!" Joelle says. "Where's the irony there?"

"I'm a virgin, too," says Cindy, "but it sounds fun to me."

Joelle puts her hands on her hips. "You don't have O/Joe waiting for you at home!" She digs around in her purse and pulls out her phone. "See? He's already called me twice and text-messaged me once today—I heart you. See that? He hearts me! How can I not go to the prom with O/Joe? He's already rented his tux! Plus, the prom's practically on my birthday! He was going to be my present!"

"You can go to *his* prom with him," I tell her. "He's got one more year, remember? This year, you have to be with us. Please, Joelle? Please?"

"If we do this," says Pam, "no one will be able to take their eyes off us. We'll be *it*, you know what I mean?"

Joelle glances at the wedding dresses. "That's probably true."

"No one's ever done this before," I say. "We'll be the first. They'll be talking about it for years."

"If I'm doing it, you can do it," Ash says.

"You know," says Pam, "you would look amazing in one of those, what do you call them? Crown things?"

"Tiaras," I say.

"You have tiaras here?" says Joelle.

"You'll have to get something lacy," says Ash. "Maybe a straight skirt."

"Sleeveless, to show off your arms," I say.

Cindy nods. "You have such great arms."

Joelle thinks about this. "Do you think I should do a veil? And maybe those white opera gloves that go all the way up past the elbows?"

I smile. "Whatever you want."

I have my friends on board, but now I need to ask my dad.

He looks up from the pile of paperwork. "You want to do what?"

"Renting the gowns will cost less than buying a prom dress. You only wear this stuff once anyway, right? Isn't that why you started the rental business? Because women didn't feel like wasting their money?"

"But they're *wedding* gowns, Audrey. Not prom gowns. Your dates will be terrified."

"We're not going with dates. We're going together. The five of us."

He frowns. "But why?"

Because, I think. *We've made mistakes and ruined things, but that doesn't make us any more horrible or slutty or sinful than anyone else, it makes us human. Because we want to make an entrance. Because we want to be beautiful, but not for a guy—for ourselves.*

I don't say any of this, though. "Because it will be cool."

"They are very expensive gowns, Audrey," he says.

"I know, Dad. We'll be careful with them. We can't

afford to rent the designer ones. We'll do the cheaper ones."

He taps the desk with his pen. "I don't know if I understand this."

There is so much he doesn't understand, and I'm tired of all that he doesn't understand. I wonder if this is on purpose, like he's mentally sticking his fingers in his ears and saying *La la la, Audrey, I can't HEAR you*, or if we've reached some sort of crossroads and there's no going back. "Do you have to understand it?" I say, tired now. "I mean, can you not understand it and let us do it anyway?"

He sighs. "I suppose I can. Are you sure this is what you want to do? Won't it spoil things for you when you go to shop for your real wedding dress?"

I snort. "I'm not going to get married for a thousand years, Dad. By then, people will be wearing tinfoil bikinis when they get married, for all we know. And anyway, we're not going as *brides*. We're like the opposite of brides. We're the anti-brides. Like nuns, only fancier. Well, not really like nuns at all, but—"

"Okay, okay," he says. "I have no idea what you're talking about, but I suppose it's fine. But please, nothing with a price tag of over $750. That will keep the rental fee down to $175, which I'll give to your friends for $125 each."

I pump my fists.

"Don't get too excited yet. Make sure your friends don't try to squeeze into any size zeros. I don't want any ripped seams. No trains; nothing too long that could drag on the ground. And I don't want these gowns coming back streaked with Gatorade or Pepsi or whatever it is you girls drink." His lips twitch and he almost smiles. "Actually, it's best if you don't eat or drink anything. Most brides don't. I mean, anti-brides."

"We'll be careful, I promise!" I say. I lean down and kiss his cheek, something I haven't done in months. "Thanks, Dad."

"Well?" the girls say, when I run back out of the office.

"He said yes!"

"Woo-hoo!" Joelle hoots, and dives for the gowns.

"Look at this," Pam says, pulling out a fluffy tulle ballerina-style dress.

"Well," says Joelle. "That could be . . . interesting."

"I want to do something totally traditional," says Ash, "and then I'll wear all this trashy makeup with it. Maybe put my hair in little knots all over my head. And a big honking eyebrow ring."

Joelle scowls at her. "I think you're missing the point."

"There's a point?" Pam says.

"I like this one," Cindy says. "The satin is so shiny!"

"I'm looking for something with a corset," says

Joelle, whipping through the dresses on the rack. "Preferably with a skirt cut on the bias so that it hugs the body."

Ash rolls her eyes.

"I really want to try this on," Pam says, holding up the nasty tulle dress.

"You can try it on," I tell Pam, "but why don't you try these, too?" I give her a halter dress with a thin line of rhinestones on the neckline, another with pink satin trim, and another plain one.

"Okay, she says. "But these are pretty boring."

I grab the shiny dress out of Cindy's hands and hang it back up on the rack. "What was wrong with that one?" she said.

"It had a rip in the back," I lie. "Here, try these. I pull some non-shiny gowns for her, some more body-hugging gowns for Joelle, and finally, some for myself. "Okay. Follow me."

We march to the fitting rooms and start trying on the gowns. Pam's first, with the tulle disaster. She flounces out of her dressing room and steps up on the carpeted block in front of the three-way mirror. Ash eyes her critically. "Cinderella on crack," she says.

Then Joelle, with one of the corset dresses she'd picked for herself.

"Mermaid on crack," says Ash.

I look at Ash, smoky-eyed and brooding in a pouffy,

lacy-sleeved number. "Black bile on crack."

We all switch gowns and try them on, then switch again. Cindy swims in the tulle dress, and I look like a dead fish in the mermaid dress. Then Pam comes out of her dressing room wearing one of the halter dresses.

Joelle says, "Oh!"

"What?" Pam says. She steps on the block. The dress is a rich, creamy white, with a plunging neckline and a full skirt.

"Wow," I say.

Pam blinks. "Wow?"

"Oh, yeah," Ash says. "That's it."

"But it's so . . ."

"Sophisticated?" I say.

"Classy?" Ash says.

"Perfect," Joelle says.

Pam doesn't say anything, but she keeps the dress on while we work on something for Ash. I run out to the rack and find the sweetest dress—white lace, Empire waist with tiny pastel flowers on it. When Ash sees it, she sneers. "Forget it," she says.

"Just put it on."

Ash strips right there, without bothering to go back into her dressing room. "This is the ugliest dress," she says, hauling it over her head.

I zip it up for her, and Joelle says, "Omigod! Ash! You're *pretty*!"

"Shut up," says Ash. She turns to the mirror and frowns.

Pam laughs. "Admit it, Ash. You look great."

"It's like a sixties dress, but like, not," says Cindy. "I love it!"

"You do?" says Ash.

"You could wear your hair all curly, but up like this." I stand behind her and scrunch her hair in my hand, letting some curls fall down into her face.

Ash inspects the little pastel flowers. "I hate flowers."

"But they love you," I say. We do Cindy next, finding her a scoop-necked, cap-sleeved gown with an A-line skirt. And then Joelle—tighter than skin, spaghetti-strapped, beaded and seed-pearled (and yeah, cut on the bias so that it skims the body). She tries on a tiara, but decides it's a little much.

"Now that we're all gorgeous," says Joelle, "it's your turn, Audrey. You wait here."

"Uh-oh," Pam says. She's still sneaking looks at her sophisticated self in the mirror.

Joelle comes back, carrying a white strapless dress with off-white embroidery on the bodice and on the narrow skirt.

"Joelle, I don't want to do strapless. I don't have the boobs for it. I don't have the body for it."

"Shut up and try it on," Joelle says.

"Do what she says or she won't leave you alone,"

Ash tells me, blowing a curl out of her eyes.

I disappear into my dressing room, pull off the dress I'm wearing, and pull on the strapless one. It's so tight that I can't zip it up by myself. I come out of the room. "It's too tight."

Joelle moves behind me. "It has to be tight so that it won't fall down. Hold your breath." I suck myself in and feel the zipper go up. "There." She takes me by my shoulders and pushes me toward the mirror. "Look at that!"

I look. I've never had anything on that fit me like this, that hugged me like this. I look like a different person: Audrey Hepburn in an old black-and-white movie.

"You know," says Ash. "That's pretty awesome."

Pam nods. "Yup. That's it."

Joelle gathers my dark hair, twists it gently in her hands, and pulls it up. "You wear it smooth, like this. See?"

Cindy lifts her A-line skirt and dances a little jig. "We are so hot!"

In the mirror, I see the tag on the dress hanging down. "Joelle, this dress is a thousand dollars. It's too expensive. I can't rent this one, my dad won't let me."

"Of course he'll let you," says Joelle. She snaps an elastic around my bun to keep it in place. "You're his daughter. You have to get some perks for that." She drops the tiara on my head and then helps me stuff my hands into long white gloves.

"I'll have to find something else," I say, touching the tiara.

"Just go ask him, dummy," Ash says. "You look great."

"I'll ask him," I say, "but he'll just say no. He didn't want me to do this in the first place."

Joelle waves her hands in a Ms. Godwin, you're-boring-me, off-with-your-head way, and I get the hint. I walk out of the dressing room and across the store to the office, where my dad sits at his desk, hunched over his paperwork. "Dad?" I say.

"Yeah?" He turns. And stares.

"I know you said that I could only rent a dress that costs under $750, but Joelle picked this one out for me and it really fits me the best. I swear I'll be careful if you let me wear it. I won't eat or drink anything. Not even water." He's still staring, and I think he's going to yell at me for messing with the designer gowns. "Dad? Can I wear it? Dad? What's wrong?"

He puts his pencil down. "Nothing," he says. He clears his throat. "You're beautiful."

"Oh." I smooth the front of my dress. "You think so?"

"Yes," he says. He stands up and leans against his desk. "Very."

I see his eyes well up and shine, and I don't know

what to do with myself.

"It's so strange to see you grown-up," he says. "I remember when you used to build forts out of the couch cushions. Do you remember that? You always got so mad when we wanted you to clean them up. You could never understand why we couldn't all sit in the forts with you. You couldn't understand why we needed a ceiling. You wanted to build those forts right into the sky."

I haven't cried once—not when the picture was mailed around everywhere, not at the doctor's office, not when I fought with Luke and realized how badly I'd messed up. But with my dad's eyes shining like that, my dad crying like that, something inside me cracks.

"Daddy," I say.

"I hope," he says. "I hope I haven't made things harder for you lately, but I think that I did. I know that I did. I was so worried for you. I didn't know how to protect you. It made me crazy."

I can't stand it. I can't stand to imagine what he thinks of me. Tears gush, streaming down my cheeks and dripping off my nose. "I screwed up, Daddy. I tried so hard to be *smart*, to be *good*, but I screwed up every-thing anyway."

"That's not true, Audrey."

I put my hands over my face, then pull them away because I don't want to mess up the gloves. "I'm so sorry," I say. "Please don't be mad at me. Please don't hate me."

He walks over to me and cups my chin, not seeming to care that I'm all slobbery. "No, Audrey, *I'm* sorry," he says. "Don't you know how much I love you?"

I shake my head, I don't know, I don't know, I don't know.

He pulls me into his arms. "You're my baby. No matter what you do, you will always be my baby."

Wearing a thousand-dollar wedding gown, opera gloves, and a rhinestone tiara, I sob myself to hiccups against my father's chest.

Here Comes
the Bride(s)

My dad insists on the full photo shoot—individual pictures of each of us, plus several thousand group shots. Even the other parents are getting impatient.

"A little camera-happy, isn't he?" Pam's mother says. She's on her second glass of wine.

My mother sighs. "I've learned not to fight it."

"Come on, Dad," I say. "We're sick of smiling. Our cheeks hurt."

"Just one more," he says. "All of you line up against the wall. Huddle together. That's it, very nice. Say 'Muenster!'"

We grin, he takes the picture, and finally we're done. Limo's already at the house, waiting to whisk us off to the prom. Five brides, no grooms. Who needs grooms? Our parents bought our corsages, roses for each of us.

We hang around my house a few minutes, getting more compliments and kisses from our parents (even though you can tell they think the wedding dress idea is less than brilliant, and quite possibly something we'll regret for-ever). My mom pulls me aside. "I hope maybe one day you'll want to wear this kind of thing for real." She hugs me tightly. "And I hope you have a wonderful time."

We totter from the house to the limo in our heels, whooping like loons when we catch my neighbors star-ing. We haven't had a thing to drink, but it's like we're all drunk.

"I can't wait to see people's faces," Pam says.

"No one is going to believe it," says Cindy. She's beaming like she never has before. She has a brand-new haircut: a bob, short and sleek. She got the idea from a book that Ash slipped her, *The Blue Castle*, by L. M. Montgomery. She says it's the most romantic thing she ever read in her life.

Joelle inspects each one of us: dresses, gloves, hair, makeup. "We're the hottest brides anyone has ever seen."

"I can't believe I'm wearing a dress with little flowers all over it," Ash says.

"And with a daisy in your hair," I say. When I say the word "daisy," I remember Luke's tiny cotton-ball dog. I figure that we'll be seeing him tonight, probably with some gorgeous girl clinging to him.

Serves me right.

Twenty minutes later, we're at the hotel. One by one, we get out of the car. We link arms and walk into the party together. As we enter the ballroom, people gape, laugh, point, grin, frown—it's exactly the reaction we wanted. I hear someone say, "I don't get it," and I elbow Ash. She and Pam snicker.

Chilly, that slimeball, grins when we pass him and his (very young) date. "Didn't think any of you ladies could wear white," he says, smirking his Chilly smirk.

Before I can think of some way to kill him without getting thrown out of the prom, Pam grins and says, "Well, well, well! If it isn't Chilly the Clown and his sidekick, Jailbait!"

We parade around the entire place, to be sure everyone gets a look at us. Then we march to find a table. We sit with two very confused couples, but we don't bother with them. We're having too much fun already.

"When does the music start?" Joelle demands. "This bride wants to shake her thang."

Pam stands up and walks around to the other side of the table. "Everyone squash together. I want to get a picture of you guys."

"Haven't we had enough pictures?" I say.

"Not here," Pam says. "Now shut up and squash."

We squash and she shoots. One of the girls at our table, who is wearing a dress with peacock feathers all over it, stares at Pam as she sits down. "What are you looking at?" Pam snaps.

"Oh!" the girl says. "I was wondering if you were in the school play? *Grease*?"

"Yeah," says Pam warily. "What about it?"

"I just wanted to tell you that I thought you were really good."

"Thanks," Pam says. She pauses a minute. "I forgot some lines in the first act. And in the second."

"I didn't notice anything like that," says the girl.

"I'm going to Juilliard," Joelle informs the table.

"We know," says Ash.

"They don't know," Joelle says, waving at Peacock Girl and company.

Just then, the DJ booms, "MAY I HAVE YOUR ATTENTION, PLEASE!! WELCOME TO THE WILLOW PARK HIGH SCHOOL SEEEEENIOR PROOOOOM!"

A cheer goes up, and Ash sneers.

"I WANT TO CALL ALL YOU LADIES AND GEN-TLEMEN OUT TO THE DANCE FLOOR TO SHOW ALL YOUR CLASSMATES WHAT YOU'VE GOT!!!"

A drum starts thumping as a bunch of people rush toward the dance floor.

"Heh!" says Ash. "You can already tell who's smashed."

"I think everyone's smashed," I say. "Or maybe they're having a group seizure."

We watched the dancing for a while.

"Don't see Luke anywhere," Ash says.

"No," I say. "Neither do I."

"If this was a movie, he'd come walking in the door without a date," she says. "Looking incredible, of course."

"Or he'd bring a date, but it would be his sister," Joelle says. "And she'd be a sad, nerdy girl we'd have to befriend. We'd have to go get her a wedding dress, too."

"Except he doesn't have sisters," I say. "He has a dog named Daisy."

"Maybe he'll bring his dog," Cindy says. "But I guess that would be weird, huh?"

"Or," says Ash, "he'd bring a date, but she'd be a big horrible bitch and end up making out with one of the football players, getting wasted, and then falling on her face in a conveniently located cake."

"Yeah," I say. "But this isn't a movie."

"Oh, *Scheisse*," says Ash.

"Yeah," I say.

"No, I mean, *Oh, Scheisse, there's Jimmy.*"

I whip my head around and see Jimmy and Cherry on the dance floor—not dancing, but yelling. "The first fight," I say. "The prom has officially begun."

"I hate that guy," Ash says. "I mean, wow. I hate him so much. And I know how to hate people, believe me. He never even said he was sorry."

"Yeah," says Joelle. "Sorry for being alive."

"And Chilly! Who *is* that girl?" Ash says. "Who would come to the prom with him? Who'd go anywhere with him? Do you think she's out of the sixth grade yet?"

Ash says, "Do you want me to go break his legs?"

I seriously consider this. The guy humiliated me, almost ruined my life, right? But then, my life doesn't really feel ruined right now. And the biggest mistakes I made all by myself. "Nah," I say. "Not worth the effort. Besides, I already decked him once."

Ash grins. "And tell me that didn't feel awesome. Think I should go smack the *Dreck* out of Jimmy?"

"Now, now," says Joelle. "Save something for later."

"You know," I say, "I thought this was a good idea until I realized that everyone else would be here, too."

"Everyone except for Luke," Ash says.

Pam swings her eyes back to me. "Have you talked to him?"

"Not since the fight we had," I say.

"But you said you were sorry." Ash says. "I mean, you *did* apologize for thinking he was screwing the planet."

"He might not have screwed the planet, but he did flirt with the planet. I had reason to be worried."

"Since when are flirting and fornication the same thing?" Pam says.

"Okay," says Ash. "He's a flirt. It's true. And that would piss me off. Still, you dumped him pretty hard. Maybe you could say something to fix things?"

"Like what?"

Ash drops her head all the way back so that she's facing the ceiling. "Please help her, God," she says, lifting her hands, "because she is so very stupid."

"Forget it," I say. "It's too late. He doesn't want to talk to me."

Cindy looks up at the ceiling. "Who? God?" she says.

"Ooh!" says Joelle. "Listen! I love this song!"

"This is a song?" says Ash.

"Shut up and dance with me!" Joelle says.

The five of us go to the dance floor and make a little circle. Joelle starts doing this thing with her hips, something that she learned in belly-dancing lessons. It mesmerizes every male within sight. Recognizing genius, Pam immediately copies it, getting it down pretty well. The two of them wiggle around in the center of our circle, and then all around the outside. Cindy is a cyclone, kicking and flailing her arms like she's in a mosh pit. Ash does her praying-mantis-shuffle-bug dance, where she pulls her elbows in tightly toward her body and jerks, keeping her feet in the same place. Of course, I don't know what I look like, but I love to dance, love it when the music is so loud you feel it rather than hear it. Like kissing Luke, it turns my brain off and lets my body take over. We wiggle and kick and shuffle for five, six, seven songs until we're all looking a little bit droopy around the edges. Then it's time for a bathroom break, where we blot and fix and adjust and admire. We hang around the ladies' lounge and make fun of everyone else's really boring, unimaginative gowns.

Joelle looks down at her sparkly, beaded, skim-the-body dress. "This was the best idea, Audrey. I mean it."

"And you didn't want to do it," I say.

"Well," she says. "I had all these birthday plans with O/Joe. But that's okay. I figured something out." She smiles wickedly.

"What do you mean?" Ash says.

"Oh, no!" says Cindy. "I'm not the only real virgin here, am I? Please tell me I'm not the only virgin."

"Don't worry," Joelle says. "I'm still a virgin. We just

did, uh, other things."

Pam leans in close. "Oh?"

"'O,' is right." Joelle adjusts her spaghetti straps. "'O' for Orgasm."

"No!" I say.

"Or. Gas. Um," Joelle says, with the emphasis on the "um." "Last night."

"How?" Ash says. "Details. Now."

"You are so touchy, Ash!" says Joelle. "Speaking of touching, . . ."

"So he fingered you?" Pam says.

Joelle frowns. "You make it sound so gross!"

"Did he or didn't he?"

"If we're being technical, yes, but it wasn't like that. We were messing around and he, you know, was trying to do *something* down there, God knows what. I took his finger and said, 'Rub. But not so hard. You're not trying to erase it, you know.'"

"Jesus!" says Ash.

Pam is smiling so wide that her face looks split in two. "How'd it go?"

"Pretty well. I mean, he did keep drifting off to the left for some reason, but after a while it worked!"

"How long's 'a while?'" I ask.

"I don't know. A half hour?"

"A half hour!" Ash yells. "Didn't his hand cramp up? Is he in a cast?"

"Hey," says Joelle, stomp-stomp-stomping. "It was *my* birthday!"

Back at the table, they're serving the entrees. We were so busy with Joelle's first orgasm, we've already missed the salad.

"What is this?" Joelle says.

I inspect my plate. "Chicken, I think."

"An animal was murdered to end up like this," Ash says. "It's so wrong."

"I'm not much for eating," Pam says. "I'd rather smoke."

Joelle pushes the plate away. "I don't want to spill any food on this dress."

Cindy, who was wolfing her mashed potatoes, puts her fork down.

We sit at the table until the DJ decides to play something decent and we get up to dance again. This time, a premature and idiotic conga line charges through our circle; Jo gets carried away and drags Ash with her. Pam, Cindy and me dance and dance and dance until we hear some commotion on the other end of the dance floor. Pam uses her elbows to get us through the crowd, though we still can't see what's happening.

"What is it?" I ask the guy next to me.

"Fight!" he shouts, and holds up a fist.

"Who?"

"Who cares?"

Then we hear someone scream: *"Will you stop it, Jimmy!?"*

We look at each other. "Ash!"

Now we're really shoving. We push our way to the front of the crowd to see Jimmy and some other guy—Nardo?—rolling around on the dance floor, pounding on each other. In a cherry-red dress, Cherry stands on the sidelines, having such a fit that her boobs threaten to bounce right out of her dress. I scan the scene for Ash. She and Joelle are a few feet away from the wildly brawling Jimmy and Nardo, and Ash is . . . smiling?

I poke Pam and Cindy and point. Ash sees us and waves like she's never had so much fun in her life, so we run around the fight to get to her.

"What's going on?"

"First," says Joelle, "Cherry and Jimmy have a spat. Cherry marches off to find herself a new dance partner. Jimmy comes over and tries to give Ash all this you're-the-only-one-for-me-huge-puppy-dog-eyes crap. She tells him to screw himself, he gets all pushy."

"Jerk tried to *hug* me," Ash says. "That's when Nardo stepped in." Her grin outdoes the Cheshire Cat's. "Jimmy got up in Nardo's face and Nardo knocked him on his butt."

Two chaperones leap into the fray and pull Nardo and Jimmy apart. Jimmy's nose is bleeding, and he's already got a shiner cooking.

"Wow," I say. "Our little Jimmy doesn't look so good."

"No, he doesn't, does he?" Ash claps gleefully, like a five-year-old at a birthday party.

As the chaperones drag Jimmy and Nardo off the dance floor, Cherry following, Ash grabs Nardo's arm. "Hey," she says.

"Hey," Nardo says.

"My hero." Ash's lashes flutter, and her voice is tiny. Ash *never* flutters, and her voice is *never* tiny. "Um, maybe you can call me? If you still want to?"

Nardo's about to faint with joy. "Yeah, okay," he says. "Tonight." The chaperones haul him away.

"Here's where Ash would say something *auf Deutsch*,'" I say. "Except Ash has been replaced by an alien imposter and we're going to have to destroy her with our ray guns."

"This calls for a cigarette," Pam says. She grabs my arm. "You come, too."

"We still have more dancing to do!" Joelle says. Ash's already bugging out to the next song, and Cindy's flailing away.

"When we get back, we'll dance the rest of the night," Pam tells her. "I swear."

I follow Pam as she crashes right through the crowd on the dance floor, ignoring the dirty looks. She cuffs

Chilly upside the head and grins when he turns to glare at her.

"That one," she says to me, "was for you."

"Thanks."

Outside, the sky is deep purple streaked with a blinding orangey pink, like flavored lip gloss. Pam lights up. "Walk with me," she says, strolling into the parking lot.

"Where are we going?"

"Around," she says. "We're enjoying this lovely evening. You want a cigarette?" She holds her pack out to me.

"Ugh. No, thanks."

We walk. She finishes her cigarette and lights another one. I wonder how many she's planning to smoke, because my feet are starting to hurt.

"I never thought I'd like you this much," she says. "I used to see you in school or at parties and I'd think, *What a priss, what a princess, what a nerd. Who does she think she is?*"

I laugh. "I didn't think I'd like you, either." I thought about what Ash said to me in the car last winter. "I guess I was kind of jealous of you."

"You thought I was a slut," she says. "Don't deny it. I heard what people said about me."

I blush, and I hope she doesn't notice. "What's a slut, anyway?" I say. "Why isn't there a name for guys who do the same thing?"

"Player. Pimp," she says.

"Please," I say. "Those are compliments."

"Anyway," she says. "I was with a lot of people. That wouldn't have been so bad if I was having a great time with all of them. Maybe there are girls who just have fun all the time—they're like boys or something. But that wasn't me. Some of the guys were bad, some were boring, some were just nothing. After a while, what's the point?"

"Well, that's why you stopped. Isn't that the point? Self-respect? Knowing what you want, blah blah blah?"

She drops her butt to the pavement and grinds it under her shoe. "I have to tell you something. You're probably going to hate me for it, and I won't blame you. I did it before I knew you."

My stomach drops and I wrap my arms around my waist. Luke. She's going to tell me she was with Luke. I wasn't wrong, I'm not wrong. But, I remind myself, it doesn't matter now. "You don't have to tell me anything."

She digs around in her purse and pulls out her little digital camera, flipping through the pictures. "Here," she says. "Look."

I take the camera. On the screen, I see Luke's naked chest, my blond hair streaked with black. I blink, not understanding. What is this doing on her camera? I don't get it, I don't . . .

Wait. "*You* took this?"

She pulls another cigarette out of her purse. "Yeah."

I realize my mouth is literally hanging open, and I snap it shut. "But why?"

"Because it wasn't fair," she says. "Everyone called me a slut, but then there you are, sneaking off with him every minute. We all knew what was going on, but no one called you a slut. No, it was just me. Cindy, too, and she's a virgin. Cindy just because she's friends with me." Her hand is shaking as she brings the butt up to her lips. "At Joelle's Halloween party, I saw you go upstairs, and I saw Luke follow you. So I went, too. I opened the door and took the picture."

"And then you sent it around to everyone?"

"Only a few people," she says.

I grip the camera tighter. "But you sent it around."

"Yes, I sent it," she says. "I told everyone that someone had sent it to me. I guess they sent it to all their friends, and then their friends sent it. Like that."

"My dad got this picture," I say. "My *dad*."

She nods. "I know."

"I can't believe this," I say. "I can't believe you'd be such a bitch."

One side of her mouth curls up, and she takes a drag on the cigarette. "Sure you can. It's why you like me."

"Like you? I want to freaking kill you!" My whole body feels hot and clammy. "Do you have any idea what you did? The notes, the e-mails, the whispering, the staring? Mr. Zwieback found this on the library computers. Mr. Goddamn Zwieback! Even Ms. Godwin thinks I'm some kind of slut now. Do you have any idea what that's like?"

But of course she knows. "I was thirteen when I first went down on a guy."

"What?" I say. I'm used to her "sassy" pronouncements about sex, but now I have no time for any of it. "Never mind. I don't want to know. I'm going back inside." I whip around and walk away, still holding the camera. Pam's behind me, talking to my back as if we were still having a pleasant conversation.

"Seventh grade. Aaron Roth. It was at his Bar Mitzvah. Funny, you know? Getting a blow job at your Bar Mitzvah. Now, there's a rite of passage."

I keep walking. She follows.

"Here's the thing," she says. "I didn't like it. I thought it was gross. But afterward, I felt so powerful. I couldn't believe that I could do that to someone else. Make them lose control like that. I walked around the party, looking at every guy there, thinking, *I could blow you and you and you and you and you.* I thought I owned them all. I thought they were mine. I thought I was the sexiest girl in the world."

I'm still walking.

"Aaron Roth did, too. For a while. And then he

broke up with me and told everyone I gave bad head. Can you believe that? If I'd been two years older, I would have smashed his teeth down his throat for saying it. But I was thirteen. And I didn't know what to do. Except maybe give more guys more head and try to get better at it. Prove I was sexy. Prove it to everyone."

That does it. I stop walking and turn around. "Are you insane? Do you really think I'm going to feel sorry for you?"

Her face is veiled with smoke. "No. I don't feel bad for me, so why should you?"

I think she's full of it, but I'm still too mad. I don't want to care about what happened to Pam in junior high. Everyone on the planet has seen this picture, this picture that *she* took, a picture that *she* sent around. I didn't do anything wrong.

"It just got to me," she says. "Everyone thought you were this nice girl, this good girl, but you were doing everything that I'd done. So why were you still good? And I'd quit guys. So why was I still a slut?" She stares off into the distance, at the lights from the hotel. "I know it wasn't your fault. I know that it had nothing to do with you. It's all me. I'm sorry. I don't know what else to say."

I think about Joelle's party, what I said about Pam, what Ash said, what Joelle said, what we all said. Pam was a whore, she'd been with everyone, she'd do anything. We said it out loud, and it didn't matter who heard.

I try to stay angry, to hold on to it. *You were humiliated in front of your parents and friends and the whole school,* I tell myself. *You had to live through Chilly taunting you and rockheads propositioning you and a doctor jamming his salad server inside you and your father shunning you.*

But, I think, even with all that, I'm okay. Partly because I have Pam for a friend.

If I was looking for irony, I found it.

"Go ahead, smash it if you want," she says, gesturing to the camera in my hand. "I'd smash it. It cost three hundred dollars and I bought it myself. If you smash it, it will make you feel better."

"It will make *you* feel better," I say.

She juts out her chin. "You want to hit me?"

"Don't be an idiot."

"You hate me, and that's fine," she says. "I was going to wait until after the prom to tell you, but I couldn't stand it. All this stuff, these dresses; asking my mom over to your house. No one's met my mom. Not even the guys I slept with."

I feel like a balloon someone's pricked with a pin, my skin slackening, my breath slipping from me. "I thought you slept with Luke," I say.

"What?" she says, her eyebrows flying up into her hair.

"I thought you were a slut and he was a player. Then Chilly told me that you guys had been together, so I broke it off with Luke."

"Chilly," she says. "I should have hit him harder. I should have taken a baseball bat to his knees."

"Yeah, well. I blamed him for this picture."

"He's a schmuck anyway." Pause. "You really thought I'd been with Luke?"

"Yeah."

"I wasn't. Ever." Her expression says it all: she thinks I'm a lunatic. "If you thought I was with him, why did you want to be friends with me?"

"I don't know," I say. "It's not like I planned it, which is so weird because I plan everything. I just did it without thinking. Then, later, I figured we had something in common. And I thought you were funny. You weren't who I thought you were." It's my turn to shrug. How do you explain those kinds of things?

"I thought *you* were funny," she agrees. "For a while, I almost forgot what I did to you. I felt like someone else, and you seemed like someone else, so . . ."

"It was us, though. We were us."

"I can just say I'm sorry. I know it was mean. Really, really mean. More than mean."

"It was," I say.

"Yeah," she mumbles.

She seems like she might cry, and I won't have any

more people who aren't supposed to cry crying; otherwise I might lose it for good. "So," I say, "while we're doing this born-again thing, this clean-slate thing, why don't you delete it?"

I hold her cigarette while she fumbles with the camera. There's a beep. "Okay," she says. "It's gone."

I nod. "Good. Let's go back inside."

We start moving, faster than before. I can feel her looking at me. "That's it?" she says, "That's all you're going to say?"

I have no idea what I'll think about this tomorrow, but tonight it's clear. "That's all I'm going to say this minute."

She takes a deep breath and squares her shoulders, so broad in that halter dress. She goes to take a drag on her cigarette, but changes her mind and throws it to the ground. "How about I take a new picture of you?"

"Now?"

She holds up her camera. "Why not?"

"Here?"

"No, on Jupiter," she says. "Yes, here."

I stop walking. "I guess."

"Stand sideways, you'll look skinnier. Oh, don't look so pissy, everyone looks skinnier sideways. Now smile." The flash is blinding.

She presses a button on the camera and shows me the photo. I see a dark-haired princess person in a pretty princess dress. Her smile is bright and sad at the same time, like the moon's.

"Who the hell is that?" I say.

Pam saves the picture and drops the camera in her bag. "I don't know," she says, "but I'll send you a copy. Maybe there are some people you could show her to."

Stars

The final class ranking: Audrey Elaine Porter, 2/314. During my salutatorian speech at graduation, I say that although I'm ranked second, I get to speak first, and that's got to count for something. I tell the audience that when I was told I had to write a speech, I had no idea what I would say; I'm more of a facts person, I'm more of a numbers person—ask Mr. Lambright, my English teacher. How do you cram the last four years into a few paragraphs? How do you make people remember from the beginning all the way to the end? How do you help everyone understand how wonderful it was and how horrible it was and how everything it was?

So, I say, I came up with a few rough statistics in an attempt to capture our high school experience in the best way I know how. In the four years we attended Willow Park High School, there were

5,600 pencils

10,000 pens

200,000 caffeine fixes

4,700 books bought

367 books sold

165 books lost

34 books stuffed in garbage disposals

13 books thrown out of moving vehicles

63,000 homework assignments

256 dogs who ate them

45,000 poor study habits

450 science experiments

162,000 unfortunate experiments with fashion

14,000 bathroom passes

15,000 hall passes

4,000 lame passes

2,800 tests passed

234,900 rumors passed

158 stupid boyfriends

143 psycho girlfriends

222 broken hearts

64,000 crazy dreams

150,000 sleepless nights

302 phones ringing

145 phones taken

3,082 tests taken

2,000,000,001 tears cried

2,000,000,001 tears dried

3,000,000 lies

5,000,000 truths

252,000 changes of clothing

45,233,000 changes of personality

141 detentions

62 eyebrow piercings

21 belly piercings

9 "other" piercings

14 tattoos

5 languages spoken

3,000 papers written

75,000 instant messages

1 too many photographs

247 games lost

532 games won

56 teachers

A trillion lessons

78 awards

3,000 friends

63,000 hugs

A zillion words of encouragement

315 success stories

Zero regrets . . .

I was told that under NO circumstances could I ad-lib it, that I had to present whatever I turned in to the principal's office for approval—a formal speech that included quotes by Thomas Jefferson, Thomas Edison, and one of the Popes—but I totally say whatever I wanted to say, and there's nothing that Mr. Zwieback or the rest of them can do about it. They don't even care; they give me my diploma and call it a day.

Plus, my speech has kicked Ron Moran's lame valedictorian ass, thank you very much.

After the ceremony, me, Ash, Pam, Cindy, and Joelle gather in the football field with our parents, congratulating one another, hugging one another, and generally being stupid and giddy. My mom and dad can't stop kissing me and telling me how proud they are, and then kissing *each other*, which normally would embarrass me to death but now seems sort of cute.

"Your parents," says Ash, laughing.

"Yeah," Pam says. "They're so happy it's disgusting."

"They're just relieved," I say. "They probably thought this year would never end. The little accident has finally graduated."

"Oh, please, Audrey. Ever since I've known you, your parents have always looked like that," Ash tells me. "They've always been happy. Face it. They're not normal."

"Don't be surprised if they spring a baby brother or sister on you while you're at college," Pam says. "They're pretty hot, you know. For old people."

I'm trying to wrap my brain around this: my parents are happy, my parents have always been happy, my parents are *hot*, when Ash pokes me and whispers, "And speaking of hot. . . ,"

Luke is standing in front of us. "Great speech," he says. With his index finger and thumb, he flicks my gold tassel and walks away before I can answer, his gown streaming behind him like a cape on a superhero.

"Who was that?" says my mom, moving to stand next to me.

"Oh. A guy I know," I say.

The guy I know shows up at my house the next day. My dad answers the door and, because of his dad radar, is immediately suspicious. Against his better judgment, he calls me down from my room.

I see that my dad hasn't invited Luke into the house; I have to go out on the porch. My dad stands behind the screen door for a minute, glowering like a guard dog. After he's gone, Luke says, "Your dad is going to get his lawn mower and try to clip me down, isn't he?"

"You run faster than he does," I say. "It shouldn't be a problem."

We sit down on the porch steps. He pulls out his cell phone, flicks it open, and shows me the screen saver. It's me in my wedding dress. The message I'd sent him with the picture said: "No, it's not a proposal, just an apology. I'm sorry for everything. I suck (and not in the good way)."

"Hot girl," I say. "Who is she?"

"Thought you could tell me."

"Can't help you," I say.

He snaps the phone shut. "Heard you guys made an entrance at the prom. Nardo filled me in."

"We did. You should have been there," I say.

"Went last year with a senior girl. I rented the tux, paid for the limo, bought the corsage, know the drill," he says. "I didn't think it would be worth it. Besides, there was only one girl I wanted to ask, and I was still mad at her."

I'm not sure what to say, so I don't say anything. We sit there for a few seconds. "What are you doing in the fall?"

"Rutgers," he says. "Undeclared major. You?"

"Cooper Union. Architecture."

"Sweet. That's in New York City?"

I nod. My heart is doing an imitation of the mambo, and my head bobs along with it. A bird calls, *Heeeeere birdy birdy birdy birdy*, and I imagine Cat Stevens salivating at the living room window.

"My grandfather's bald," Luke says suddenly.

"Huh?" I say. "Random much?"

"My brother's losing his hair, too."

"Your brother? Which one?"

"Jeff."

"But he's only, like, twenty-two or something!"

"I know. He's freaking out. So's Eric. It runs in my family. My mom's dad was bald by the time he was twenty-eight. Her brother was only twenty-five." Luke puts a hand on the top of his head. "I figure I should enjoy it while it lasts, you know? That's how I think about a lot of things. You should just enjoy them. I mean, maybe I'll be bald next year and maybe I won't. I can't worry about it now. Do you know what I'm saying?"

Great. Metaphors. That's what I need in my life, more metaphors. "I'm not sure."

"We had a good time, didn't we?"

The heat rises in my cheeks. "Yeah. We did."

"Well," he says. "Except for the dumping thing. And the treating-me-like-I'm-some-sort-of-leper-horndog-for-practically-the-whole-year thing."

"Except for that. I'm sorry about that."

He doesn't answer; he just props his elbow up on his knee, his chin in his fist, and gazes at me—like he's already moved on, like all of it was something that happened a decade ago and why get all worked up over it? I think about how he tried to go down on me that one time and maybe I could have let him—it might have been okay, it might have been . . . nice. But then again, maybe it would have been a disaster. I hadn't trusted him. I didn't know him. I didn't know myself.

He bumps my shoulder with his. "I guess I shouldn't worry about losing my hair. You wanted me for my body, anyway."

"Watch it. I can always get my dad again," I say. "I'm

pretty sure he's in the kitchen, sharpening his knives."

He laughs. "Touched a nerve?"

"You touched all of them," I say, picking at my fingernails. "The nerves, I mean." I feel so stupid, sitting here. He's been inside me and I've been inside him. I've swallowed his spit, his sweat, and he's swallowed mine. How do you talk to a guy after that? How do you *start* talking to a guy after that?

"You told me once that you'd read *Moby Dick* and you thought it was funny."

He nods. "Yeah, I did think it was funny. Why?"

"What else?" I say.

"What else what?"

"What else should I know about you?"

"Let's see. I'm five foot ten and weigh 162 pounds. I like dogs, moonlit walks under the stars, and milkshakes I can share with that special someone."

"You are so not five foot ten."

"You can check my license." He picks up my hand. "You seeing anyone?" he asks me. "Nardo—Ash—said you weren't."

"No," I say. "You?"

"Gave it up for Lent." He runs a finger in the spaces between my knuckles. "I told my mom I'd bring the van back by six today, but do you want to go to the beach tomorrow?"

I'm surprised. "The beach?"

"Yeah, the beach. You know, sand, water, bathing suits. I'll do my best to win you a really huge, really ugly stuffed animal on the boardwalk. On the way, you can ask me all the questions you want."

"I don't know," I say.

"Come on," he says. "It'll be fun."

I think, *Yes!* I think, *No!* I think, *There's no way this will work. I'm still me and you're still you—I'll obsess, you'll flirt, we'll go down in flames.* I think, *I'm leaving, you're leaving. Rutgers is too big and New York City is too big and there's too much to do and too many people to meet. We're seventeen years old and eighteen years old, we'll come home older and won't know who we are anymore, as if we ever did. Maybe it's better to leave it where it is, while we don't hate each other . . .*

"Hey," he says, giving my hand a squeeze. "Stop it. Stop thinking for one second. We have the summer. You can't know everything that's going to happen."

"I—"

"You *don't* know everything."

He's right. There are a billion things I don't know, as this year has proven. Why not take a chance? We do have the summer. Two whole months of it.

"Come on, Audrey." He drops my hand and holds his up like I've pulled a gun. "I'll keep my mitts to myself, if that's what you want."

I admire his long fingers. They look strong, like they could last a while, a half hour maybe. But I'm more greedy than that. There are other things I want, too. His brain, maybe even his heart. I'll start with those and see what happens. "Okay," I say. "The beach it is."

He smiles. "I'll see you tomorrow, then. Ten too early?"

"No. I'll be ready."

"Good," he says.

He hops down the stairs and takes the driveway in a jog. Then he turns around and runs back.

"Forget something?" I say.

"Yeah," he says, and leans down and kisses me—short and sweet. A casual, friendly, see-ya-later kind of kiss, the kind we never got to have before.

After he's gone, I sit there a long time, watching the clouds form and re-form, feeling the warm breeze, the kiss on my lips, just trying to be still, just trying to *be*. It's hard, being. Hard not to pit yourself against yourself, hard not to measure and compare and rank yourself against everyone else. It'll take practice, and I'm not sure if it will ever work. Then I remember some dumb saying, or maybe a song, about having the same sky over us and the same stars shining down on us and the same God smiling with her big God teeth, and think now that it's corny, but true. Our moon is the same moon, our sun is the same sun, and the stars will sparkle for us no matter who or where or what we are—not sluts, not players, just people. We can all look up and say, *Okay, there's the South Star, there's the Big Dogpile, there's the Little Dipshit.*

Twinkle, twinkle.

Acknowledgments

Thanks to my editor, Clarissa Hutton, who was willing to take a chance when I wanted to write something completely different. Ellen Levine, who is equal parts agent and fairy godmother. Anne Ursu and Gretchen Moran Laskas, who push and prod and occasionally, prop me up—every writer should have such amazing friends. The 2005 Writefesters, especially Greg Leitich Smith, Cynthia Leitich Smith, Tanya Lee Stone, Libba Bray, and Sean Petrie, who braved both the first draft and my near-psychotic fretting over it later. Audrey Glassman Vernick, who kindly lent criticism, support, and her first name. Carolyn Crimi, Esther Hershenhorn, Myra Sanderman, Esmé Raji Codell, and Franny Billingsley, who can take one cranky writer and make her laugh so hard and so long that she (almost) forgets how to be cranky. Melissa Ruby Horan, Annika Cioffi, Linda Rasmussen, and Tracey George, who have listened for years and for some crazy reason, keep on listening. My parents, who let me read everything I could get my hands on and answered every question without blushing. And finally, thanks to Steve, one of the good boys.

Good Girls

Laura Ruby dishes on *Room Raiders*, Judy Blume,
and how stealing can make you a better writer

Ash tries the writing thing in her very own story, *Pepper Nuts*

A sneak peek at Laura Ruby's upcoming novel *Play Me*

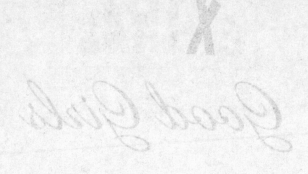

Forget the Rumors

NOT YOUR MOTHER'S Book Club grills the author on everything from what inspires her to why Wonder Woman would beat the Tooth Fairy in a fight.

NYMBC: The usual question first. What was the inspiration for *Good Girls*?

I'm not really sure. One minute I was sitting at home, doing what I normally do—that is, talking to the cats—and the next minute I'm thinking, geez, our culture is weirdly obsessed with sex.

I know, I know—this is news? But all of a sudden, I was sick of it all—the *Girls Gone Wild* ads, songs that call women bitches and hos and really mean it, *Room Raiders*, Paris Hilton tapes, porn stars everywhere, blah blah blah. I thought, What's going on here? Has an evil cabal of thirteen-year-old boys taken over the universe?

It seemed to me that though we're obsessed with sex, we don't really like to talk about it, not in any realistic way, not in context. So, we settle for all this fake stuff. And the point of a lot of the fake stuff seems to be to make girls feel like crap.

Again, nothing new. I remember being confused and angry about sexual double-standards when I was back in high school. But what's different today is the technology—cell phones, instant messages, texting, etc.—that makes communication so quick and easy. Of course it also makes rumors spread faster than ever before (as if they needed any help). It has also caused a strange erosion of privacy that I find kind of creepy. I wondered what would happen if a regular teen, a "good" girl, was a victim not only of the ages-old sexual double-standard but also of the technology we rely on so much.

NYMBC: I consider this book essential reading for girls (and also parents and teachers). Seriously. But you know there are going to be some people who freak out about the content, probably without even reading it. So, did that worry you at all while you were writing it? Did it affect the way you tackled the story?

Well, that's the funny thing. I knew people would be freaked out about the subject matter, but I wrote the book because I was freaked out! Still, I tried very hard not to think about any of that while I was writing it because I wanted to be as authentic as I could be. There was no point in writing anything less than that. Only after the early drafts were done did I examine whether or not certain situations or language was necessary to include.

NYMBC: So, do you think that the gap between the generations (especially in terms of how they view sex) is really greater than it has ever been, or do you think that teens and parents just THINK it is?

One of the reasons I wrote this book was not because things have changed so much since I was a teen, but because things haven't changed enough. Sure there are differences, like the technology I mentioned earlier. But so many of the feelings and the assumptions are the same; Judy Blume's *Forever* is still relevant and that was written more than thirty years ago!

NYMBC: Indeed, I still love *Forever!* What sort of assumptions do you mean, though?

We still act as if guys have no emotions and girls have no desires of their own. I don't think these attitudes have served any of us very well. Actually, I think they've helped to create this surreal porn-land we seem to be living in.

NYMBC: What did you like to read when you were a teenager?
Everything! I loved Paula Danziger, S.E. Hinton, Lois Duncan, Norma Klein, Robert Cormier, and especially Judy Blume. But I also devoured everything Stephen King wrote, went through a brief romance novel phase, and stole all my mom's mysteries. Edgar Allan Poe was an early favorite, as was Shirley Jackson. I liked the dark stuff. Still do.

NYMBC: Me too! What, if any, other jobs have you had besides writer?
Babysitter. Library clerk. Sales clerk. Waitress at a restaurant called Stuff Yer Face. Advertising copywriter for a company that made "collectibles" such as porcelain busts of Jesus.

NYMBC: Not so glamorous! Speaking of not-so-glamorous jobs, we've got a lot of members who like to write. What advice would you give to a teenage aspiring writer?
There's the usual—read everything you can. And then the not-so-usual—steal everything you can. By steal, I mean listen carefully to what people say, the kinds of stories they tell and the way they tell them, and then steal all of it for your work. (I always ask before I steal, though. It's only polite.) And if they won't give them to you, then you might have to change the stories enough so that they can't recognize them.

And that's my third bit of advice—lie.

NYMBC: Quick-fire challenge, Ladies' Edition: Who would win in a fight—Wonder Woman or the Tooth Fairy?
Wonder Woman. Hello, Magic Lasso!

NYMBC: Cleopatra or Queen Elizabeth I?
Elizabeth. You didn't see her killing herself with an asp when the Spanish got uppity.

NYMBC: Amelia Earhart or Katharine Hepburn?
They would never fight, merely bond over a mutual affinity for pants.

NYMBC: Hello Kitty and Little Twin Stars or Josie and the Pussycats?
Depends . . . if it's Josie the cartoon, it could be a fair fight. If we're talking the live-action Josie and the Pussycats, Hello Kitty would kick their butts.

NYMBC: Annie Oakley or a she-bear?
One thing I've learned in life—always bet on the bear.

Thanks to Jennifer Laughran, Not Your Mother's Book Club, and Books Inc. for allowing us to reprint this interview.

Pepper Nuts
by Ash

So, the story's done. The end. *Finis*. Everyone drives off in a giant pumpkin and lives happily ever after, right?

Right.

"Ach! Bumblebees again!"

This is Grandma Franke talking, but not about bees. We're making pfeffernuesse—spicy German cookies. I'd asked her if we could make chocolate chip, but Grandma Franke doesn't like chocolate chip. Also, Grandma Franke doesn't like little metal boxes that buzz.

I pat my pockets while she glares, leaving flour handprints all over my pants. My cell's in the pocket down by my knee. I flip the phone open and read the message:

miss u

I never thought I needed anyone to fight my battles for me, but something about Nardo taking on Jimmy . . . I don't know. I lost my head. I told him to call me. That was weeks and weeks ago. I thought maybe we'd hang out for a little while, and then he'd get bored and drift off. Or I'd drift off. Someone always drifts off, which is what I keep telling Audrey.

She laughs and says, "It doesn't look like Nardo's going anywhere."

And I guess he's not. He calls every day. He shows up at the ice-cream shop, where I'm scooping for college money, and always brings me something weird. A shiny rock, a paper clip bent into the shape of a swan, the Teenage Mutant Ninja Turtles spoon his mom said

7

was his favorite when he was a baby. And then there was this:

> Roses are red
> Beets are purple
> You're never sweet
> But that would be boring.

"It's my first poem," he told me.
"Really," I said.

Now Grandma Franke looks over my shoulder at the phone. "What's that thing say?"

"He misses me."

"He who?"

I open my mouth to say Nardo, but then I look at the number. "Jimmy." Just saying the name makes my mouth feel dry. And then I'm pissed that my mouth is all dry, because I'm supposed to be over Jimmy. And then I'm pissed that Jimmy is texting me. And then I'm pissed because I'm a little bit happy that Jimmy's texting me. It's the second time this week. If she knew, Audrey would remind me how much happier I am with Nardo. Joelle would threaten to ram her purple suede boot down Jimmy's throat. Cindy would say that it's so romantic to have two guys fighting over me. And Pam would smash Jimmy's kneecaps with a tire iron.

I toss the phone on the counter. "What's wrong with me, Grandma?"

She grunts, dumping melted butter and honey into a mixing bowl. "Too many gadgets, not enough cookies." She beats in some eggs and adds some drops of anise—her secret ingredient—while she has me sift baking powder, cinnamon, ground cloves, mace, all-spice, and a bit of pepper in with the flour. When I was little, I thought it was weird to put pepper into cookies. Grandma Franke said it made perfect sense to put pepper into cookies called pfeffernuesse. She said that anyone could make chocolate chip, but it took a little magic to make pepper nuts.

She tosses the flour mixture into the bowl with the butter and honey. Then she thrusts that bowl at me. "Mix," she says.

"Can't we use the mixer Mom bought you?"

"*Nein*," she says, though she doesn't need to say it. Grandma believes electric mixers make the cookies taste fake. She watches me struggle to mix the thick batter. "You're getting weak."

I *am* weak. I can't help looking at the phone on the countertop.

"Staring at it isn't going to help," she says.

"What would help?" I say.

"Throwing it in the trash," she says.

"I can't throw it in the trash. I need it."

"*Ja*. Like I need bedbugs." She takes the bowl back and gives the dough some strong German twists with her strong German arms. Then she puts the bowl in the fridge to chill.

"So which one was it?" she says, jabbing a finger at the phone. "The good one or the bad one?"

"What?" I say. "How did you know?"

She laughs. "There's always a good one and a bad one."

"It was the bad one," I say.

"I thought so."

9

"He's a liar," I say.

"Ja."

"And a cheater."

"Ja."

"And a complete jerk."

"Ja, ja."

"But he won't get out of my head."

She wrings out a sponge in the sink and wipes the countertop. "That's the way with the bad ones."

"Why does he do it?" I say. "Why does he keep showing up wherever I am? Why would he text me when he knows I'm with Nardo?"

"Because he knows it will make you *verrückt*. The bad ones always want to make you—"

"Crazy," I say. "But he dumped me for someone else. He doesn't even want me."

"He wants you to pine away for him. He's like those chocolate chip cookies. You eat and you eat and you're still starving."

We wait a half hour for the dough to chill in the fridge. Then we take it out, roll it into balls, and bake. The whole kitchen smells like a spice store. Like Christmas.

After the cookies cool, we dust them with powdered sugar. Grandma Franke pops one into her mouth. When she's done chewing, she says, "The good ones are like pfeffernuesse, *ja*? Sweet and spicy at the same time. They have their own bite. Full of surprises."

I think of Nardo, his insane gifts, his stupid poem, the way he will sometimes grab me and kiss me before I even know what's happening.

Grandma loads up a plastic container with the cookies. "And the longer you keep them around, the better they taste."

This makes me blush. I try to hide it behind my hand but Grandma Franke sees everything. She hands me a cookie. "You have to decide. You want a chocolate chip that anyone can have? Or do you want a pepper nut? Something special, just for you?"

I bite into the cookie. I can taste everything—the honey, the cinnamon, the cloves, even the pepper. Sugar and spice and surprises.

I smile.

"That's my *liebling*," she says. "Always the smart one."

"Now I just have to get Jimmy to stop texting me," I say.

Grandma Franke seals the container of pepper nuts. "Why would you want to do that?"

"But you just said! He's the bad one."

"*Ja*," she says. "That's why you let him buzz you, but you never ever answer. Let him pine away for you this time. Let *him* starve." She drops the last pepper nut into the container and snaps the top down.

I shake my head. "I think *you're* a little bit bad, Grandma Franke."

"Pfeffernuesse," she says, patting my cheek. "Just like you."

**A sneak peek at Laura Ruby's
upcoming novel *Play Me*,
set at the same high school as *Good Girls*.
WHAT HAPPENS WHEN A PLAYER GETS PLAYED?**

PLAY ME
Laura Ruby

Most people turn into complete morons when you put them in front of a camera, and thank God for that.

Today I've got the digital trained on the two guys in my driveway—one on a unicycle, another on a tall bike. They're getting ready to joust. Their pages (pimply dorks with anime-brain) hand them their lances (poles made from PVC pipe). Duct-taped to the ends of the lances are huge stuffed animals, an Elmo and a Hello Kitty. The object? To ride straight at your opponent and Elmo him right onto his Hello Kitty. And if you knock him hard enough to cause a) bleeding, b) broken bones, or c) a humiliating, painful, and yet strangely hilarious groin injury, that's even better.

It's one of the dumbest things I've ever seen and I'm so happy. Watching these guys strap on bike helmets decorated with flaming skulls, I have to keep from doing my own moronic dance of joy.

"This is going to rock," Rory says, fiddling with the

boom mike he's setting up to catch the walla walla of the crowd gathered in the garage and in the yard. We're shooting for our show, *Riot Grrl 16*. Our riot girl, Gina, is in full costume: black cherry lipstick, pink and black hair spiked as high as she could get it, striped shirt, and camos. Her feet are bare, but her pants are rolled up so that you can see the tiny tattoo of an ivy vine on her calf. (I told her once that it would be good for the show if she got a dagger tattooed somewhere; she said that the best place for a dagger was my heart.) In this scene, she's supposed to be partying at a tall bike joust when her drug-addicted brother shows up claiming to be in deep with the mob. Instead, Gina's busy leveling her patented Death Glare of Obliteration at me. I'm not sure of the reason for this, but since the Death Glare looks good on camera, I don't care.

Rory's still fiddling with the mike. "Are we going to get any sound or what?" I say.

"Keep your panties on, princess." He built a mile-long boom with multiple joints so we can get the thing almost anywhere, and we've never had it drop into the shots. He also built the steady cam. And we have a dolly that he rigged up from the Segway Gina's richer-than-J.K.-Rowling parents bought her, the one they said would help her be a more environmentally responsible human, the one she called "the Dorkway." But today, like most days, we're using handheld, held—of course—by me.

"Okay," Rory says. "We got sound."

A groupie hovers to my left. She's standing so close I can feel her breath on my arm. She's a junior at my school, but I keep forgetting her name. She's hot, if you like legs that go up to there. (And who doesn't?) She's been hanging around our shoots for weeks now.

"It's so cool that you guys are in this contest," she says. "I mean, YTV is even bigger than MTV now. Can you believe it?"

Yes, actually, I can. "It's pretty cool."

"It's awesome! What will you do if you win?"

"We're just trying to make the top five and get on the prime-time broadcast," I tell her. "That's enough visibility for us." This is the standard answer I give so I don't sound too full of myself, even though I think *Riot Grrl 16* is the best in the contest and people would be insane to think otherwise.

"Oh, you'll totally make the top five," Groupie says.

"You think so?"

"I know so." Groupie's lips are nice. Puffy and full. Lips you could use as throw pillows. "I've been watching you," she says. "You know your way around a camera."

I shrug. "I should. I've been doing it for long enough."

She nibbles at her puffy bottom lip and flutters her lashes. "I heard you know your way around a lot of other things, too." It's a lame line, but her voice is low and scratchy and hits me right in the fly. I calculate how fast I can hustle twenty-five tall-bike-riding geeks out of my yard.

"Jeez, can you focus for three seconds?" Joe says. Joe doesn't believe in fame, commercial success, or groupies. My mom told me that one day Joe will be forced to do a TV ad for foot fungus cream just to have the work and won't be so proud.

"Hello?" says Joe, doing that slow-blink thing he does when he's annoyed.

"I'm focused, I'm focused," I say. I can't help it, my eyes are drawn back to Groupie's up-to-there legs.

Joe snorts and whispers something to Gina. Gina is making some kind of snarling sound and jabbing fingers in my direction, so I hurry up and center the shot.

The two jousting goons start racing toward each other, both of them wobbly as six-year-olds. I love it. For a minute, I forget about the groupie, I forget where I am, I forget everything that's happened in the last year and revel in the idiocy that unfolds before me. Tall Bike completely misses his opponent, but Unicycle gets in one good whack. Tall Bike looks a little dazed, at least more dazed than when they started. They circle around for another run. Charge!

Groupie wraps her hot little hand around my bicep.

And Gina launches a bottle at my head.

"Ed! Duck!" Rory yells. Too late, as usual. The bottle misses my face but bounces off my arm. My father's tools explode off the pegboard where they'd been arranged like a row of exclamation points.

"Hey!" I say, not because of me, but because of my dad's tools. My dad hates when his stuff gets messed up. He'll kill me when he sees it. Okay, he won't kill me, but he'll make me pay for it, which might as well be killing me because I'm broke. I spent everything I had on the new video camera. Speaking of, what if she'd hit it?

It takes me a few seconds to notice that Gina's crying; she wears so much makeup that it's sometimes hard to tell if the effects are intentional. "You're such an ass," she says, her lips quivering.

Rory shakes his head, which tells me he thinks *Riot Grrl 16* isn't acting, she's running riot for real. Behind her, the jousting continues. It's not looking good for Unicycle.

"What?" I say, reframing the shot so that Gina's in the foreground with the joust behind her. "Who's an ass?"

"And you can put the stupid camera down," she says, glancing around the garage for more ammunition. I lower the camera.

Joe throws up his hands, picks up his Bible, and flops in one of the folding chairs in the garage to wait this little episode out. He hates any drama that we don't create for the screen. And Gina is drama personified. She's spitting out an array of impressive and colorful swear words, which, if she wasn't saying them so fast, might have an impact. Right now, she sounds like she's shouting in Latvian: *mutherfushiheadasdik!*

I'm getting impatient. We do one episode of *Riot Grrl 16* a week. We have till tomorrow to finish it and get it up on the Web, otherwise we'll be disqualified from the contest. We really don't need to have our star freaking out on us, not unless she'll let us post it on the Internet.

"Gina," I say. "Can we talk later?"

"We can talk *now*!"

Rory quietly pulls his own digital camera out of his pocket, the one with the video capability. I know he's going to film this. It's wrong, but I don't mention it. I had to promise lots of screen time to these guy to get them to joust at my house instead of at the park; we should have something to show for today. Besides, I'm missing all the action in the driveway. Unicycle went down. No embarrassing groin injuries, but it appears he did fall on his face, which now sports a few racing stripes. Two new guys are setting up to joust, one of them with fat, matted dreads snaking down the middle of his back. White guys should never, ever, *ever* wear dreads, especially while riding a tall bike with a SpongeBob strapped to the handlebars.

"What's the deal with her?" Gina says.

"What's the deal with who?"

This is not the right thing to say.

"Her!" Gina bellows, pointing at the groupie. "Ms. If-Her-Shorts-Got-Any-Shorter-They'd-Be-A-Gynecological-Exam."

This has got to be about what happened three or four weekends ago. We were rehearsing for *Riot Grrl 16*. Dad out for the night, working late as usual. So, yeah, things got a little out of control, but not in a bad way. I thought Gina was cool with it.

I guess Gina's not cool with it.

She's really crying now, the black mascara or eyeliner or greasepaint or whatever it is that she puts on her eyes dripping down her cheeks and onto the striped shirt. I like Gina, we're friends. I don't want to see her so sad.

Rory really shouldn't be filming this.

"Gina, look, I'm sorry," I say. And I am. Yes, we hooked up, but I didn't promise her anything. I didn't think she needed any promises. I mean, she'd even hooked up with Rory once.

Then something else hits me and for a second I can't breathe. I take two steps toward her and try to lower my voice (for all the good it does). "Wait. You're not, like, late or anything, are you?"

Gina's mouth drops open.

Joe's mouth drops open.

Even Rory's mouth drops open.

It would have been funny, if things weren't so very unfunny.

"Dude," Joe says.

Gina starts to laugh then. Some kind of crazy-creepy laugh. Sort of scares me, that laugh.

"No, I'm not *late*, you loser. But even if I was, I'm not sure I'd tell you anyway."

"So what are we fighting about?"

"You just don't get it, do you?" she says.

And you know what? I *don't* get it. What I do get is that the first episode of *Riot Grrl 16*, the one we did just for kicks even before the contest, was one of the featured videos on YouTube. It got more five-star ratings than the skateboarding dog, the guy who stuffed a dozen olives up his nose, *Top Ten Ways to Die in a Video Game*, and *The Best Banana Phone Video Ever*! And what I do get is that Gina has completely lost it the way that girls always seem to, the way they do when you least expect it. It's like they wait until you're at your most stressed out and then they lay this weird trip on you, like you all of a sudden had more going on with them than you had. What is up with this? I just stand there, staring at her, watching her cry and laugh at the same time, wishing I could maybe hug her or something, but I know I can't touch her.

CPSIA information can be obtained
at www.ICGtesting.com
Printed in the USA
LVHW042241040221
678412LV00005B/30